"I'll bet there are plenty of people who'd have been glad to bash her brains out if they had the chance." She tipped the empty glass to her mouth again, sucking at the ice. "Not that I'd expect you to admit it, being such bosom buddies. But a lot of people hated her guts, take it from me."

Lee wisely resisted two impulses: first, to come to Kate's defense; second, to ask where Dorothy had heard this oddly prevalent rumor that she and Kate had been so close. Instead she put down her wineglass and asked coolly, "Anyone in particular?"

Dorothy glared at her and set her glass down with a thump. "My advice to you," she said flatly, "is to stop playing Miss Marple, or whoever it is you're supposed to be, before you find *yourself* dumped in a lake or something."

Also by Aaron Elkins:

Curses!*
Old Bones*
A Deceptive Clarity
Murder at the Queen's Armes
The Dark Place*
Fellowship of Fear*

**Published by Fawcett Books*

A WICKED SLICE

Charlotte and Aaron Elkins

FAWCETT GOLD MEDAL • NEW YORK

A Fawcett Gold Medal Book
Published by Ballantine Books

Library of Congress Catalog Card Number: 89-30086

ISBN 0-449-14686-3

This edition published by arrangement with St. Martin's Press

Manufactured in the United States of America

First Ballantine Books Edition: December 1990

With sincere thanks to Cobe Holmstad, golf pro at the Nile Temple Golf Club, Edmonds, Washington.

1

NEVER FRET OVER a poor shot. Dismiss it from your mind and get on with your game.

Oh, sure.

Lee stared accusingly at the dimpled golf ball peeping with such smug innocence from the tangle of iceplant. The old rule made sense, but not fretting was a lot harder when it was your seventh wretched shot of the day.

There were always a few rotten shots, of course; that was part of the game. But she had never had this kind of trouble with slices before. The small, good-humored segment of the gallery that had started out with her had shrunk to an edgy knot of four or five by the fifth hole. By the seventh they'd melted away altogether, slinking shamefacedly off to follow more likely prospects, and who would blame them? Her fairway game had come apart at the seams, and nobody wanted to watch a supposedly grown woman do likewise.

It was unbelievable. She had felt good entering the Pacific-Western Women's Pro-Am Tournament, and on Monday she had shot a blistering 68 in the qualifying round. But today . . . she was too embarrassed to look at her three dejected amateur partners, who had each paid $2,500 for the privilege of playing three rounds of competitive golf with a competent pro . . . but who had wound up with *her* instead.

In reproachful silence her caddie handed her the six-iron she'd asked for. Poor Lou had to be wondering what he'd done to get stuck with her and how she'd ever qualified for the tour. And Lou wasn't the only one. Lee was starting to wonder too. Slices, yet.

Resolutely she cleared her mind and concentrated on the next shot. The most direct route to the green was blocked by the thick, gnarled trunk of an oak about twenty feet in front of her. No doubt Arnold Palmer or Sandra Haynie would have driven the ball over it (or through it), but this was emphatically not Lee Ofsted's day for heroics. The most she could hope for was to chip laterally out of the rough and back onto the fairway. She brought the club concisely back, swung firmly, and managed to punch the ball out of the clutching vegetation and back on to the short grass. Even better, she got a fine roll on it so that it didn't stop until it reached the middle of the fairway, giving her a clear line to the green, a soft nine-iron away.

"Hey, great shot! We really popped it out of there!" The sudden grin on Lou's dour, monkeyish face was so delighted, so genuinely astonished, that it made her feel worse than ever.

"We're back on our game now, no sweat," he said, sliding the iron into the big new Hogan bag that had cost her an alarming $170, but what choice did she have after the bottom literally fell out of the old nylon one?

"Bop a few more beauts like that," Lou went on with uncharacteristic verbosity, "and the last few are gonna be smooth sailing; no sweat. Smooth sailing," he chirped again as they trudged from the sand dunes that edged the dogleg on Carmel Point's eleventh hole. "No sweat."

Did he really have to lay it on quite so thick? He was trying to raise her spirits, of course, but it sounded an awful lot like wishful thinking. Or praying.

Which is what it turned out to be.

Lee's unaccountable fairway-wood slice earned her a bogey on the fourteenth and a mortifying double bogey on sixteen—or it would have been mortifying if any fans had stayed around to watch—giving her a miserable 80 for the day. Still, she told herself, with two more rounds to go before the final cut, there was a good chance to make up for it. All she had to do was play the best golf of her life for the next two days.

No sweat.

When she finally plucked her ball out of the cup on the eighteenth green, she straightened up, nodded grimly to her partners, and turned to see Nick Pittman moving nervously toward her. Anxious faces on tournament officials—especially Nick—were nothing unusual, but this one looked serious. Nick even forgot to make the standard polite query about her round. Or maybe he already knew her score and was too gentlemanly to bring it up. Either way was fine with Lee. Her golf game was the last thing she wanted to talk about. The sudden development of a hook wouldn't have been so embarrassing, but everyone thought of a slice as a hacker's problem, not a pro's. And everyone was right.

"Where's Kate? Have you seen Kate today?" Nick asked, falling in step as they walked toward the clubhouse through a crowd paying Lee no attention at all. There wasn't even a kid who thought enough of her to ask for her ball.

"Kate O'Brian?" She shook her head. "Anything wrong?"

"Yes, there's something wrong. She didn't show up for her starting time, that's what's wrong."

"Didn't show up—" Lee stopped momentarily. "Then she's disqualified?"

"She sure is. We had to move up the top nonqualifier to take her place. Wilma Snell." Nick's plum-colored lips jerked at the corners. "Can you just imagine what that's going to do to our TV ratings? The sponsors are furious. Who the hell ever heard of Wilma Snell? Oh," he said awkwardly, "pardon me."

"That's okay, Nick." She understood what he was apologizing for. Who the hell, after all, had ever heard of Lee

Ofsted? But at least she had survived the qualifying round on her own merit.

Nick was shaking his head. "Kate's pulling out isn't going to do anything for the gate either."

No, it wouldn't. Kate O'Brian was a sensational golfer with a flamboyant, roistering personality that might have been designed for television. She had been the center of attention at any tournament she chose to enter for the last fifteen years. And "chose" was the right word. As a top money winner she could afford to pick and choose the tournaments that caught her fancy. No competing in the qualifying rounds every week for Kate O'Brian. Unlike some golfers who came to mind.

A mild jab of concern nudged her. "You know, that just doesn't sound like Kate. It's hard to believe she'd casually drop out of a tournament without saying anything."

"Yes, yes, I know." Nick waggled his head in agreement or consternation. "And the Sawyer people are fit to be tied. She was supposed to do an interview this morning for their *Golf World* show, and she didn't show up for that either."

"Oh, no. Milt Sawyer must be hysterical."

"He is, he is. Hysterical," Nick agreed, and the thought seemed to settle him a little. Even hysteria loved company.

Nicholas Shapeworthy Pittman III reminded her of a country squire, if you could believe the old movies; a big, beefy, outdoorsy man of fifty who looked as if he belonged in a tweed shooting jacket, jodhpurs, and boots. Riding to hounds. His face in repose was probably twinkly and self-complacent, but Lee had never seen it in repose. As chairman of the board of directors of thc Carmel Point Golf Club, he had wound up with the thankless and impossible job of tournament director for the first Pacific-Western Women's Pro-Am, and now he sported a nervous tic under his right eye, carried around a shirt pocketful of Maalox tablets, and the hunted look of a man who knew it was only a question of time until the next unimaginable disaster.

Or it could be he'd always looked like that.

Nick walked a few more steps. "Lee, I don't know where

the hell she *is*!'' he said abruptly. ''Where *is* she? *You* must know!''

''Me? How should I know?''

A fresh set of furrows seemed to settle into Nick's forehead. ''Well . . . aren't you her best friend?''

Lee blinked with surprise. ''No, I'm not.''

''Well, somebody said you were,'' he said reprovingly.

''Well, I'm not. I'd like to help, Nick, but she never said anything to me about it.''

And why should she have? In point of fact, Lee knew Kate—really knew her—hardly at all, despite the long, talky drives they'd shared in the last few months.

Even if Kate hadn't turned out to be a surprisingly private person away from the limelight, it would have been difficult for the two of them to spend much time together. Kate was a bonafide superstar, while Lee was on the bottom rung of the touring professional's ladder—one of the ''rabbits,'' so named because they survived, if at all, by nibbling at what was left over after the big-time players got done carving up their shares of golf's green rewards. Some were first-year pros like Lee herself; others, more desperate, were older players whose games were erratic or slipping away.

For Lee the Women's Professional Golf League tour was an endless series of once-a-week rushes to the next town on the circuit to nab a room in a Motel 6—or whatever chain was offering discounts to players—before all the other rabbits snuffled their way there. Otherwise she was likely to wind up sharing a room with someone who watched TV until 4 A.M., or snored, or popped funny pills, or used her toothpaste.

Breakfasts were Egg McMuffins; lunches were Big Macs or all-you-can-eat-smorgies (except when free meals could be scrounged); dinners were best not described. Entertainment consisted of long, hard, sweaty sessions on the driving ranges or, more often, because they didn't cost anything, the practice tees.

Kate O'Brian lived in a different world. For her the tour was all five-star restaurants and luxury hotels, with interviews on "Good Morning, America" sandwiched between the golfing and the glittering parties at somebody or other's gorgeous home on the seventh fairway.

"I mean, I know her," Lee said, "and she's been nice enough to give me some lifts between tournaments, but we don't see much of each other once we arrive." They didn't see each other at *all*, except on the course.

She paused at the shoe-cleaning device near the clubhouse door and scrubbed her left shoe against the brush to get rid of the stubborn caked earth. (That would have been from the sixth hole, where, with her luck running true to form, her third stroke had landed on the muddy rim of the laughable little water hazard just to the right of the green.)

"I ran into her at the practice tee last night," she said, frowning down at the mud-stiffened leather, "and she didn't say anything about pulling out of the tournament. In fact, she was practicing. She was working with her irons."

"I don't know," Nick said. "I just don't know."

While Nick went worriedly off to pry what information he could out of others coming off the final hole, Lee carefully cleaned, dried, and creamed her shoes at her locker; they were going to have to last the month no matter what, and she didn't want them falling apart like the bag. Then she showered, considering what to do next.

Ordinarily there wouldn't be anything to consider; she would take advantage of one of the first-day buffets that opened their doors to anyone in the tournament. But for once she didn't feel like eating, even for nothing. The news about Kate had made her uneasy. Besides, her dismal round was enough to kill her appetite by itself. With play like that she was going to have a hell of a time making the cut and getting into the final rounds.

It wasn't merely the tournament prize money she was hoping to share in, not that that wasn't important; the longer range implications were more serious. Another cut missed in her freshman season and her pro career would be over before it was fairly started.

No, work was what she needed, not food.

* * *

Carmel Point's 230-yard practice hole was one of its showpieces, framed on one side by the layered cypresses that clothed much of the Monterey Peninsula and on the other by a graceful, curving lake that echoed the lucid blue of the ocean a quarter of a mile beyond. At another time, in another situation, Lee would have been elated at the idea of a week in one of the world's most spectacularly beautiful places. Not only was there no other spot quite like this green and rugged chunk of land jutting into the Pacific a hundred miles south of San Francisco, but nowhere else were there four golf courses of such quality in so small an area: the celebrated Pebble Beach, Cypress Point with its fabulous sixteenth, the fiendishly frustrating Spyglass Hill, and the newcomer, Carmel Point, co-hosting its first major tournament with the other three.

But it wasn't another time or situation, and she could have been in the middle of the Utah salt flats for all the pleasure she got from the scenery. At least she had it to herself, no doubt because all the other rabbits were busy munching away at the buffet table and sneaking rolls into their pockets.

She decided to go directly to the source of her problem and pulled her three-wood out of the bag; her trusty three-wood, usually so reliable in getting her to the green in two on the par-fives. She started with basics, checking her grip, stance, and address before carefully taking the club back. All okay, as far as she could tell. Her take-away was unhurried and low along the ground, the swing itself rhythmical and smoothly accelerating, driven by the coiled strength of her hips and shoulders. Just like a rock on a string, as the golf magazines were so fond of saying. At the snapping release of her wrists the club face smacked the ball so firmly, so satisfyingly, that she might not have known she hit it except for the solid, unmistakable *s-h-h-o-o-k!* of a golf ball perfectly struck. She closed her eyes gratefully. Whatever had been so wildly wrong this morning, it was all right now, thank God; a passing aberration. She was back in form. She opened her eyes.

The ball sliced.

She watched it disbelievingly, shading her eyes with her hand, as it arced to the right in a long, lazy parabola; farther to the right and then farther still, until it dropped 190 yards away, missing the lake by a few feet.

"Golly, Lee, didn't that ball slice?"

Lee's eyes rolled upward. Just what she needed, a helpful observer. She turned with a stifled growl to find a puffily overweight man of thirty-five, with pale, strawlike hair and a dollop of white sun cream on his nose, peering earnestly at her. Milt Sawyer, self-styled bon vivant and confidant of the rich and famous. And eager dispenser of dubious golf advice.

"I think I know what you're doing wrong," he announced predictably.

Lee managed a smile. "What's that, Milt?"

"You're picking up the club head too soon on the back-swing, so you're losing that right-elbow tuck." He beamed indulgently. "I once told the same thing to Bernie Langer when he was going through that bad patch last year and he's still thanking me."

Whether Bernhard Langer was really in his debt was highly doubtful, but with something like a five handicap, Milt was a pretty fair club golfer, and maybe he had something. But Lee was like most pros: She knew her own game, and she resisted the well-meant tidbits of advice that people tossed so freely around golf courses. Start tinkering piecemeal with your swing, and you could wind up in real trouble. It had happened to a lot of good golfers.

"You could be right," she said, maintaining the smile. "Have you found Kate yet?"

"That's what I wanted to ask *you*."

"Sorry, I haven't seen her." With her club Lee nudged another ball into position.

Milt's near-transparent eyebrows knitted. "Then it looks like we'll just have to go with someone else on *Golf World*," he said petulantly and delicately probed at his zinc oxide-lathered nose with a stubby forefinger. This seemed to reassure him.

"You know, Arnie owes me a few favors. So does Seve.

Maybe it's time to call them in. If not, I can always ask Juli or Amy. Or maybe Muffin; she'd be good." He wagged his head. "But I wish Kate had just let me know."

"I'm sure she had a good reason for not showing up," Lee said. "Did you try getting in touch with her manager? He's around somewhere."

"Farley?" Milt emitted something between a snicker and a snort. "He's worthless. He doesn't know where she is either, and she's supposed to shoot another spot for us tomorrow. We already have studio time booked." He frowned and his voice took on a husky reverence. "Gosh, Lee, we're talking contractual obligations here. I remember the very first time I met Lee—Lee Trevino, I mean. We were having drinks in the Champions' Lounge, you know, at La Costa, and Lee said that a contract—"

"Kate's probably trying to get in touch with you right now, Milt," Lee cut in. "Maybe she's already called the WPGL. You might want to try the tent and see." She took her stance, settling in behind the ball, hoping that Milt might get the message.

He didn't, of course. He just stood there, pudgy hands jammed morosely into the pockets of his yellow-and-blue-plaid, double-knit trousers.

Milton Sawyer was the son of Ellis P. Sawyer and the Executive Vice-President and Publicity Director of Sawyer Sports Equipment, which provided Kate O'Brian with a lucrative contract to endorse their golf products. Once, on one of their long drives, Kate had rambled on wishfully about not renewing the arrangement. The regional television commercials linked to upcoming events were an increasingly embarrassing chore ("Does Kate O'Brian use Sawyers? You bet I do, honey! Just ask me at the Krispy Kookie Open, in your area June third to seventh. Here's how to get tickets.") Besides, Kate had said, it would be worth giving up $110,000 a year not to have to go to any more lunches with the name-dropping, self-inflating Milt, who was by all odds the most excruciatingly boring person in the world, according to Kate.

Lee had told her *she'd* be willing to be bored for $110,000, and Kate had laughed. "Keep improving and you just might, kid. Keep the amount to yourself, though, will you? According to the contract, compensated endorsers aren't supposed to talk about their compensation." She'd switched to an English accent. "Bad form, don't y'know."

Since then Lee had learned from personal experience what Kate had meant about Milt. Fifteen minutes after accepting his spur-of-the-moment dinner invitation the night before, she would have been comatose if she'd actually been trying to listen to his endless self-puffery instead of merely supplying him with occasional polite cues. Not that he needed much prompting. Fortunately the prime rib and roasted potatoes at the Monterey Hilton were more than capable of holding her attention, particularly inasmuch as they were the first meal since the morning's Dunkin' Donuts Special.

"Well, I'll certainly let you know if I see her," she said, wriggling more pointedly into her stance. It was hard for her to dredge up much sympathy for the fleeting problems of the heir to the Sawyer fortune—even if he was beset by inanity, fatness, and a much-bemoaned inability to tan evenly.

"I'm afraid I'd better get back to work," she added firmly.

This time the message got through, but barely five minutes after Milt had shambled off toward the nearby clubhouse, Lee heard a golf cart jouncing along the gravel path in her direction. She kept her head down, concentrating on her ball.

"Hi there, Lee!" someone called amiably. "How's the slice coming?"

Wonderful. More company. Lee sighed and rubbed a hand over her forehead. It hadn't been her morning, it didn't seem to bc her afternoon, and she was reluctantly coming to the conclusion that it wasn't going to be her day. When in the world was she going to get a chance to put in an hour's uninterrupted work on that slice? Probably tomorrow morning at 7 A.M., she thought gloomily, when it was barely light enough to see. There wasn't much going on out there at that time.

Frustrated as she was, it was hard for her to be rude. Especially to one of the amateurs in her foursome. She raised her club in greeting and smiled wanly. "Hi, Peg."

Peg Fiske was stocky, talkative, and lively, with a voice like a bugle and deep laughter creases around her eyes, and they'd hit it off reasonably well considering their awkward introduction the day before. Lee had been in the check-in line behind Peg and couldn't help overhearing:

"Which pro's going to be in my group?" Peg had rumbled cheerfully.

"Well, dear, let me see . . ." The woman at the trestle table moved her pencil uncertainly down the list.

Peg helped her along. "Pat Bradley? Betsy King? Kate O'Brian?"

"No. . . . Let's see, I don't . . ."

"Nancy Lopez? Jan Stephenson, maybe?"

"Ah," the woman said with satisfaction, "Fiske. You should have told me it was with an 'e.' Your pro is . . ." She adjusted her bifocals with one hand and leaned over the sheet. "Your pro is, let me see, Dee Ofsted. No, it looks like 'Lee.' Lee Ofsted. Or would that be 'Oaf-steed'? I don't know how it's pronounced. It's Scandinavian, apparently."

Peg was silent for a moment. "Who?"

"I'm sorry, dear," the woman said, ready to move on to the next person. "I don't make the assignments, you know. It's not my fault."

Peg shook her head sadly and addressed the sky. "Where do they come up with these people? One of these days I'm going to get someone I actually heard of."

The woman offered a routine sympathetic cluck and looked over Peg's shoulder at Lee. "Name, dear?"

What could she do but grin and say "Ofsted. Pronounced 'Off-sted' "?

Peg had been flustered and embarrassed, but by this morning she'd recovered, and by the time the round was over, Lee found that she had enjoyed the woman's company. Peg was a management consultant whose approach to golf was annoyingly mechanical but whose blunt good nature more than made up for it. Her ready sense of humor had made Lee smile even on her three bogeys. On the double bogey nothing could have made her smile.

"Well," Peg said now, "have you licked that dumb slice?"

"No." Lee leaned on the club. "Did you get a look at the scoreboard? How are we doing?" Not that she really wanted to hear.

Peg hooted with laughter. "Last I saw we were already lying twenty-eighth in the field, as they say, with most of the scores yet to come in."

"Ouch. Well, there's no point in worrying. With thirty-six holes to go before the cut, anything could happen."

"Sure," Peg said brightly, or as brightly as her foghorn of a voice would allow. "Like the first twenty-seven could get hit by lightning."

Lee watched as Peg unzipped her shag bag and shook three or four dozen pristine balls onto the worn grass. Top-of-the-line Titleists . . . for practice!

With a sigh Lee used the head of her club to set up ten of her own scarred balls; "X-outs," mostly—factory seconds that the manufacturers sold at a discount, but only on the shamefaced condition that a stamped string of X's hide the brand. Ah, well, her time would come.

If, that is, she could work her way out of this miserable slice. She lined up, looking down at the ball, out to the spot 210 yards away that she was aiming for, and back to the ball. She took a preliminary waggle, all the time conscious of Peg's open interest. It was flattering that her partner thought she was still worth watching after this morning, but then Peg hadn't had much of a round either. Instead of playing in the low nineties, up to her eighteen handicap, she had ended with a 105, for an adjusted score of 87. If not for the steady play of the other two amateurs, they'd be lying a lot lower than twenty-eighth.

Lee had been too concerned about her own game to offer advice beyond the choice of a club or the reading of some of the trickier greens. Besides, it was pretty clear after a few holes that Peg suffered from one of the weekend golfer's most debilitating maladies: She was *too* willing to take advice—from pros, from caddies, from onlookers, from anyone who wanted to give it. Every time she flubbed a shot she changed her stroke, or her stance, or her grip to suit some quickie cure she'd seen in a magazine.

Maybe Lee would be able to help her yet before the tournament was over; at least she might be able to convince her to find her own style and stick with it. But first things first.

One more look at the limp yellow flag, then down at the ball again. Press, pull the club back, launch the hips, let it go.

Damn, it was unbelievable. A slice, a fat one, curving sneeringly off to the right toward the lake. Lee groaned inwardly. As nice as she was, if Peg said "Wasn't that a slice?" or anything remotely like it, she was going to get the club wrapped around her throat.

Fortunately for them both, the older woman just frowned and looked honestly concerned. "Does it bother you to have me watch you?"

Lee lined grimly up to another ball. "Uh-uh. That's not my problem."

"Do you have any idea what your problem is? Identifying the problem is two-thirds of the solution."

Lee shook her head and doggedly took her stance. She didn't want any management consulting techniques applied to her golf game.

Unsurprisingly, Peg persisted. "Would it help—I mean, tell me if I'm bugging you—but would it help if you told me what you were working on and I gave you some feedback on whether you were doing it?"

Lee relaxed her stance and shrugged. It couldn't hurt. "Sure. Basically, I'm just trying to make sure I stay relaxed and keep my swing smooth."

"Right, what else?"

"Well, I guess that my timing isn't jerky."

"Check. And?"

"And . . . and that's all. I suppose I want to make sure I stay square to the target," she added to satisfy Peg.

"You're kidding me."

Lee looked inquisitively up from the ball.

"I *mean*," Peg said explosively, "if you're slicing, shouldn't you be making sure your hands aren't too far to the left? And your club face isn't open? And your swing path isn't outside-inside? And your wrists aren't breaking early? And—"

"Peg," Lee laughed, "if I tried to remember all that I'd go bonkers."

"But . . . but . . ." Peg floundered for words. "You *have* to keep all those things in mind when you swing. Otherwise—"

"Not me," Lee said. "I step up to the ball, and I try to stay relaxed. And I hit it. That's it." She smiled crookedly. "Of course, after this morning maybe I ought to—"

Peg dismissed this with a wave of her hand. "No, today was just an off day. The fact is, you're one of the best few hundred golfers in the world, a card-holding touring pro—"

"Just barely," Lee muttered.

"—and all you think about when you swing is to . . . just to . . ."

"Relax and belt it," Lee said apologetically. "I guess the rest sort of comes naturally. Most of the time."

Peg's good-natured face came as close as it could to rancor. "That," she said, "is disgusting." Without further conversation she began to line up her own balls ten or twelve feet away.

That suited Lee, and with a sigh—she seemed to be sighing a lot today—she went back to work, trying hard not to think about early wrist-breaks and outside-inside paths. The first swing felt good, an effortless, fluid transfer of power from hips, to shoulders, to snapping wrists, to the whipping club head. Her hands finished high and elegant, the way they should, and she kept her head down an extra fraction of a second before lifting it to look for the ball.

For a moment she thought it was going to be all right, but at about 140 yards the clean, true arc began to disintegrate, and the ball slid sideways and dropped into the sky-blue lake with a pretty little splash of white.

And suddenly, for the first time, she was genuinely, deeply disheartened. She just didn't know how to hit a golf ball any better than that. Fifty swings later, with a good many practice balls she could ill afford to lose resting on the lake bottom, she was numb, actually thinking about chucking it—not just the Pacific-Western, but the whole golfing career she'd so naively decided on for herself.

After Peg finished working on her drives and went off to the bunker to practice sand shots, Lee slogged over the grass toward the lake, armed with her telescoping-handled ball retriever. (Would an honest-to-God pro even own such a thing?) What on earth was driving her anyway? Who gave a damn whether she made it or not? She had no backers except Cobe, who would just as soon have her work off his $6,000 loan in his pro shop and on the range at the North Portland Public Golf Course.

Well, she thought morbidly, with no room in the credit card accounts, a depleted checking account, and only two weeks of expense money left, the question of whether she "decided" to continue playing would soon enough be moot.

A couple of balls were visible within easy reach of the shore, and those she scooped up with her hand. The coolness of the water was a refreshing surprise; she hadn't realized how warm she'd gotten flailing away on the tee. On a whim she tossed her shoes and socks onto the grass, rolled her pants up to the knees, and stepped out onto the squishy mud of the lake bottom. If she were reduced to dredging her old practice balls out of the lake—and all right, yes, anybody else's old practice balls she happened to come across—she might as well enjoy herself. God knows there hadn't been many other whimsical impulses to give into that day.

It had been a long time since the lake had been cleared. There were balls all over the place, and all she had to do to find them was to part the reed patches with the handle of the retriever, or simply go squelching around until she stepped on one. In ten minutes she found fifteen, which was three more than she'd lost, and if some of them were on the spongy side, how much did that matter for practice with the driver?

After a few more minutes, however, she had stirred up a cloud of mud, and soon the knee-high water was too murky to see through. She would have to quit with a net profit of six balls, which made it the day's most successful enterprise.

She turned to wade back to the shore, gingerly placing her feet in the mud.

But not gingerly enough.

"Ouch. . . . *Damn!*"

She jerked her foot out of the water with an indrawn hiss of breath. A cut foot was all she needed to contend with in tomorrow's round. Leaning awkwardly over with her right foot propped against her left knee, feeling like an unstable stork, she anxiously examined the ball of her foot. No blood, thank heavens, and no broken skin. Only those peculiar indentations, almost like a set of . . .

She looked more carefully. Spike marks? Had someone thrown a show in the lake? She'd heard of—she *knew* of—golfers who had thrown whole bags of clubs into water hazards in fits of rage. But a *shoe*? She bent and used her hand to feel for it. Yes, spikes. And there was the heel. A shoe, all right. But why so heavy? Or was it stuck in the mud? She tugged.

By the end of the day she would ardently regret her well-intentioned reaction to the horrible discovery that the shoe contained a foot, that the foot was attached to a leg, and so on. What she did was to drop to her knees and try to drag the body out. With jumbled, fragmented memories of stories about people who had been revived after being submerged for many minutes, with the thought-paralyzing fear that she wouldn't remember how to administer CPR when it came down to it, with a brackish, heaving stomach—and the dazed, mindless certainty that she somehow knew exactly what she would find—she scrabbled frantically with her fingers, trying to get hold of a handful of clothing, trying to avoid the cold, repellent, rubbery flesh.

Slipping and unable to get a foothold, she slid under the surface herself for a nightmarish moment, for the head lay downslope in about four feet of water. She must have called out then, because suddenly Peg was at her side. Together, with Peg's voice rolling over her in unintelligible waves, they dragged the body close enough to shore so that the head and throat lay exposed.

Still on her knees in the water herself, Lee fell back on

her haunches and let her eyes tremble closed. She'd never seen a dead body before, but there wasn't any doubt about this one, and the horrible cup-sized depression in the waxy forehead made it all too apparent that death had not come by drowning.

And, yes, she'd been right. It was Kate O'Brian.

2

"YEAH . . . YEAH . . . OKAY, Good. Thanks, Fisher." Captain Bushell pressed down the receiver button with his left hand. The telephone remained cradled between his shoulder and his ear while his pen continued to scribble over the sheet. When he hung up, he thought for a moment, walked from his paneled office to a glass-partitioned cubicle beside it, and plopped his hefty bottom into a chair beside a desk at which a sandy-haired man of thirty pored over a police report folder.

"Hey, Sheldon, what do you know about golf?"

Lieutenant Graham Sheldon, four months with the Carmel Police Department, looked up from the malicious mischief report that he'd been reviewing. ("Vandal or vandals unknown allegedly cut a two-by-two-foot hole into F. A. Zoppo's wire goose enclosure, allowing two of said geese to escape from property at . . .")

"Golf?" he said. "Well, I know you have to chase a little ball around and hit it in a hole with a stick, and you're supposed to wear funny clothes while you're doing it—purple stretch pants with yellow checks and white shoes. Oh, and a white belt."

"Good," Captain Bushell said. "An expert. Just what I need. Got something for you at the Carmel Point course. Something big."

"Wow, somebody must have siphoned some gas from a golf cart."

"Funny," Bushell said, eyeing him quizzically. The captain hadn't quite figured out what to make of him, Graham knew; hadn't decided whether he was a good cop, or whether he even liked this big-city boy wonder with all the commendations who had come out number one by a mile on the detective lieutenant exam. Which had made it impossible to promote Rubio, who'd been a sergeant with the department for thirteen years and had counted on the job as his. Rubio with his five kids.

"No, it's a murder," Bushell went on evenly. "How does that grab you?"

Graham didn't quite know how it grabbed him. He had quit Oakland PD and taken the job with the Carmel mainly because seven years of metropolitan sleaze and violence had left him repelled and disgusted. No, that wasn't quite true; it had brutalized him more subtly than that. It was when the endless, savage thuggery had *stopped* disgusting him that he knew he'd been there too long. It had started to seem like the normal human condition to him, and he'd begun to see in himself the cynical contempt for people—that is, for people who weren't policemen—that was so common in longtime cops. And that was a hell of a way to feel for someone who'd come out of Berkeley as a starry-eyed do-gooder with a *cum laude* M.A. in sociology not so very long ago.

But after four months in this beautiful seaside city of Carmel, he'd discovered to his surprise that he missed it; not the grunginess and horror, of course, but the police work itself, the resolute, dogged persistence demanded by criminal investigation, the satisfaction—rare but all the sweeter for it—of putting the really bad guys away.

"All in all," he said to Bushell, "I'd say it beats the hell out of goose-napping."

As far as he could tell, it didn't do much to ease the captain's mind about him.

* * *

Graham leaned back in the soft leather chair behind the manager's desk he'd commandeered in the office next to the pro shop and looked at the freshly dried but still bedraggled young woman staring back at him from her seat. Everything about her set his teeth on edge: her deep, even, country-club tan; that WASPish way of moving—graceful, lithe, athletic, as if she owned the place, the not-so-subtle alligator on her trendy golf shirt, now mud-streaked and clinging. Well, maybe that part didn't set his teeth on edge.

He knew he was being unfair. Country-club rich plus country-club beautiful didn't necessarily add up to arrogant and obstructive. No more than eight times out of ten, in his experience, but he couldn't help the way he felt. Probably a result of those two miserable summers he'd put in as a busboy at Oak Bluff Golf and Racquet Estates when he was trying to scrounge enough money to put himself through Cal. In any case, he wasn't counting on getting a lot of useful assistance from Lee Ofsted.

Too bad it hadn't been the one he'd just interviewed, the sturdy, down-to-earth Mrs. Fiske, who'd found the body. She'd have had the good sense to leave it undisturbed.

"I know you've gone over all this with Officer Fisher—" he said.

"Three times," she murmured.

"—and I know you've been here a long time, and you've had a tough day, but I'd like you to run through it one more time, please."

He'd expected a litany of grievances and complaints, but she only nodded docilely and began to tell him, hesitantly, in that surprisingly soft voice of hers. Could he actually have lucked out and run into one of the two out of ten?

He waited patiently until she'd come to a breathy halt. "Let me ask you something, Miss Ofsted. Why didn't you simply call the police in the first place? What made you haul the body out?"

At the word *body* she shivered. "I thought that maybe I

could revive her, I've had CPR training, and I thought . . ." She shrugged weakly.

He shook his head. "The lake was in your sight for the whole time you'd been on the tee, right?"

"Yes."

"All during the time you'd been practicing."

"That's right." Her voice was hardly audible.

"And during the time you were talking to Elizabeth Fiske and Milton Sawyer."

She nodded.

"Half an hour, would you say?"

"More or less."

He leaned forward. "So what you're telling me is you intended to revive someone who'd been underwater for at least thirty minutes and almost certainly longer?"

Under that creamy tan she colored slightly, showing signs of spunk for the first time. "People have survived after being submerged for as much as an hour, Lieutenant," she said crisply.

"In icy water, yes. Not in a sunny pond on the Monterey Peninsula in September."

"Oh." She dropped her eyes, the pluck draining visibly from her. "I guess my flopping around has disturbed things for you, hasn't it?"

"No, not really."

No more than if a herd of hippos had used the place for a watering hole, but he didn't have the heart to tell her that. What would be the point?

"I'm sorry," she whispered. "I suppose I wasn't thinking very clearly."

"Look, Miss Ofsted," he said more gently, "I know how hard this is. We'll be done in a minute, and I'll have someone get you to your hotel. Just a few more questions."

She raised her eyes.

"You finished up your day's play this morning, is that right?"

Lee nodded.

"Well, then, what were you doing out here this afternoon?

Just playing for fun? I'd have thought you'd like a break from golf."

To his astonishment she burst out laughing. "I was practicing, not playing. And I certainly wasn't having fun. Golf is a deadly serious business, Lieutenant."

His eyes strayed to a small ceramic figure on a corner of the glass-topped desk: a six-inch-high golfer wearing purple pants and an orange beret complete with white pompon. He was bent over from the waist, parting a thicket with his club and peering into it. Behind him an alligator's jaws emerged from the painted water.

"Old golfers never die. They just lose their balls" said the imitation-brass plaque on the base.

"Yes," he said without expression, "I suppose it is. Tell me, how well did you know Kate O'Brian?"

Lee shrugged. "About as well as anyone else on the circuit—which wasn't very well. Kate's given me some rides between tournaments, but she always made a point of keeping her work and her social life separate."

"And when did you see her last?"

"Yesterday, a little before dinnertime."

"Four o'clock? Five o'clock? Six o'clock?"

"Well, it would have been a little after five. It was right there, on the practice tee, actually. I'd been at it since about four-thirty when she came along to put in some work on her long irons."

"By herself?"

"Yes, or at least I didn't see anybody else. I was just going to the clubhouse to get a sweater, and when I got back she was gone."

"How long were you away?"

Lee shrugged. "Twenty minutes or so, I guess. I had a quick cup of tea at the clubhouse."

"Didn't that strike you as a pretty short practice session for her?"

"Well, the fog was rolling in and the visibility was zilch. I knocked off too as soon as I got back to the tee. If you can't see where your ball's going, there isn't much point. You can't make corrections."

"Where was your caddie? Surely you weren't picking up your own balls."

He was angry with himself as soon as he said it. What right did he have to be snide with her? She was utterly defenseless, she was vulnerable, and she was being as cooperative as she could. It wasn't her fault if the creeps at Oak Bluff had given him a hard time.

"I suppose," he said before she answered, "somebody comes around and picks them up later."

"On the driving range, yes, but not on the practice hole. The golfers use their own balls there, and their caddies usually pick them up."

"But not last night?"

"No, I was doing it myself. I'd . . . I'd worked out an arrangement with Lou for him to start full-time caddying for me the next day—that is, today—when the tournament started." After a second she added, "I don't have a permanent caddie."

"And Miss O'Brian's caddie? Where was he?"

She frowned. "I don't know. I hadn't thought about that. Ben usually carries for her but he wasn't there." She paused. "It's funny now that I think about it, because I saw him near the clubhouse earlier in the afternoon. Maybe she wanted to work on something by herself. That happens sometimes."

"Ben who?"

She shook her head, embarrassed. "I'm afraid I don't know. You can find out from the caddie master."

"All right. Now, when you got back to the tee with your sweater there was no one in sight at all?"

"No, I told you—" She paled very convincingly and came to an abrupt halt. "Do you mean that's when Kate was killed? That while I was drinking my tea someone . . . someone . . ."

The leather swivel chair squeaked as Graham straightened. He leaned his forearms on the glass-topped desk. "I don't know," he said truthfully. "That's what it looks like, but we'll find out for sure when we get the medical examiner's report."

Lee slumped and blew out a long, wavering breath. "My God," she murmured dreamily, more to herself than him, "if I hadn't gone away, she might still be alive." Her green eyes weren't focused on anything in the room. "It wasn't that cold; not really. I didn't really need a sweater. If I'd just stayed a few more minutes, only a few more minutes—"

"—you might be dead too, with both your bodies still at the bottom of the pond," Graham said. Brutal, but it did the job. She blinked, shivered, and returned to the present.

"Did she say anything about meeting anyone later on?" he asked.

Lee shook her head listlessly.

"Did she seem upset about anything?"

"No," she said hollowly. "She just seemed like Kate."

Graham studied her. She might be back in the present, but she was about at the end of her rope, and who could blame her? Dragging dead bodies from lakes would be pretty horrifying stuff for someone with her rarefied background.

Not that great for someone with his either.

"I'll probably have to ask you some more questions later, Miss Ofsted," he said, and noted with interest and some surprise that the thought no longer set his teeth on edge, "but I think we can call it quits for now. Can I arrange a lift anywhere for you?"

"No, thank you," she said quietly, and surprisingly managed a small, sweet smile of gratitude. "Peg said she'd give me a ride."

The smile got to him. Where the hell had he gotten the idea that she thought she owned the place? Damn, he hated it when people messed around with prejudices that had stood him in good stead for years.

"Where can I get in touch with you if I need to?" he asked. "Are you staying at the Pebble Beach Lodge too, with Mrs. Fiske?"

"Am I—?" He had the odd impression she might have

giggled if the circumstances had been different. "No," she said soberly, "I'm at the Motel 6 in Seaside."

He waited until she'd stepped out of the room and politely closed the door behind her before permitting his eyebrows to ride up.

Motel 6?

3

GRAHAM WAS STILL staring bemusedly at the door when there was a tentative knock. He started, wondering if she'd come back.

"Come on in," he called.

It was Sergeant Rubio, looking nervous, which didn't particularly worry Graham. Gerald Rubio always looked nervous.

"Okay, I got what you wanted," he said, "but it's a mess."

"Ah," Graham said, but his expression must have shown he had forgotten what it was he wanted.

"A list of everybody who had access to the practice tee?" Rubio reminded him. He frowned darkly at the Big Chief writing tablet in his hand. "You're talking about a lot of people."

"How many?" Graham almost smiled. Rubio had a constitutional need to make mountains out of molehills. But not this time.

"One thousand three hundred and seven."

Graham let out a whistling sigh. "Thirteen hundred people had access to the practice tee? I thought it was closed to the public."

"And seven," Rubio corrected. "There are a lot of people

involved in this tournament, and anybody with a tournament pass could have got on to the tee."

"I know, but—"

Rubio consulted the top of his tablet. Graham could see that it was covered with his microscopic handwriting, straight up-and-down and maddeningly neat. "Okay, we got a hundred and sixty-eight amateur players and fifty-six pros. They all have caddies, two hundred twenty-four of them, and then we got another seven hundred and fifty people helping run things, mostly volunteers from around here."

Graham's chair whooshed as he sank back into it. "Opportunity" was not going to be his best lead. "It takes seven hundred and fifty people to run a golf tournament?" he said weakly.

"According to Nick Pittman, it does," Rubio said a little defensively, "and he's the tournament director, so he ought to know. For starters, you have to have four marshals at every hole, two at the tee and two at the green, just to hold up the 'quiet' signs. So that's four times eighteen holes, which equals seventy-two. Then you got forty-five different committees: a scoring committee, a rules committee, a public relations committee . . ." He paused to flip to the next page. ". . . a gallery control committee, a liaison committee, an awards party committee—"

"I get the drift, Gerald."

He had noticed before that Rubio, a small, darty man with a jet-black widow's peak and a perpetual scowl of wary anxiety, was nearest to tranquillity when he was armpit-deep in details and paperwork. He would have made a hell of an accountant, Graham thought, not for the first time. Or a police lieutenant, he might have said before this murder had come along to tear him away from Farmer Zoppo and the missing geese.

"And don't forget," Rubio cautioned him, "about the twenty-three reporters, forty-five club employees, and forty-one WPGL officials and sporting goods reps. Any one of them could have been out there on the tee. All together, one thousand—"

"—three hundred and seven," Graham said with a sigh. "Have a seat, Gerald."

Rubio slipped into the chair Lee had used. He was wearing a dark-blue suit, a white shirt, and a gray tie with tiny red fleurs-de-lis. He dressed like an accountant too. "Where do we go from here, Graham?" he asked, scowling.

There had been a time, just after Graham had joined the force, when he'd worried about Rubio, who had, after all, been an unsuccessful candidate for the lieutenant's slot and was now subordinate to the man who'd taken it away from him. But he'd quickly found that what he'd thought to be resentment was merely Rubio's normal state of uneasy anxiety. Sergeant Rubio, he'd finally come to understand, was immensely relieved not to have gotten the promotion, and considered himself in debt to Graham for appearing out of nowhere to spare him the burden of increased responsibility and authority.

"Beats the hell out of me," Graham said cheerfully. "I think I'll go see what Davis has to say."

When he opened the door of the office he was startled by a microphone that was thrust at him so abruptly the foam cover bumped his teeth. The pro shop was bursting with ill-humored and impatient reporters and TV cameramen, most of whom were gesticulating at him and all of whom were shouting. He ducked back inside the office and quickly slammed the door.

"Whew. Why didn't you tell me about that?"

"You said you didn't want to be bothered with the press."

"I don't, but I guess Kate O'Brian is big news. Look, will you get on the phone to Captain Bushell and tell him we'd better put out a release, and that we need an officer to handle press relations, because if he thinks I'm going to do it he's out of his mind."

"Uh . . ." Rubio's worried face shrank with increased concern.

"What's the matter, Gerald?" Now there, he mused, was an enlightening difference between the two cities he'd worked for. Was there a cop on the Oakland force who would willingly answer to "Gerald"? (In his Oakland days Graham had cravenly resorted to his middle name, getting by with "Tom.") This distinction between the two police departments was not necessarily to Carmel's detriment, in Graham's opinion.

"Well . . . do you really want me to tell Captain Bushell that?"

"You can just tell him"—Graham laughed—"that it would be administratively expedient to appoint someone to direct press relations inasmuch as Lieutenant Sheldon's time is fully occupied in the assiduous performance of his criminal investigative responsibilities."

"That I'll tell him," Rubio said with a rare smile of his own, "if I can remember it."

Graham put his hand on the knob. "Okay, I'm giving it another try. Look through the window, and if you don't see me make it to the outside within five minutes, send in the SWAT team to get me out."

He pulled open the door and burrowed through the mob, head down, mumbling "no comment" at every second step. When they tried to follow him out the back door of the building and around the temporarily barricaded gravel path that led to the practice tee, he turned and held up his arms. "I'm sorry. No farther, please."

As expected there were moans of outrage. "Who the hell are you?" somebody called angrily.

"I'm sorry," he repeated politely. "We're just not ready for you yet. Sergeant Rubio is talking to Captain Bushell right now about getting someone here to fill you in. You'll just have to be patient a few more minutes."

He turned and walked toward the tee, listening to the cursing behind him. They would have been surprised to know that he'd enjoyed those gruff "no comments" and the brief exchange that had followed. Four months on the job, and this was the first time anything bigger than the Carmel *Pine Cone* had shown the least interest in anything he'd been doing.

At the small lake just off the green, about 180 yards from the tee, the regional crime lab team from Salinas was packing up their metal suitcases, chatting amiably and pouring themselves coffee from a plastic jug. One of them was sitting on the bank, cigarette dangling from the corner of his mouth, laughing quietly at something someone else had said and peeling off armpit-high rubber waders. They might have been a friendly fishing party wrapping up a lazy afternoon at the pond, if not for the arcane equipment being neatly tucked away—and Kate O'Brian's body, lying on its back on the grass under a three-sided tent that protected it from the sun and from the curious eyes of the reporters in the clubhouse and the gawkers trying to peer through the cypress stand to see what they could from Carmel Way, almost a quarter of a mile off.

A quarter of a mile. Was it possible that the killer hadn't been one of Rubio's one thousand three hundred and seven after all, but an outsider who had managed to get in? True, the course was fenced—at least this part of it was—but security wasn't exactly up to San Quentin standards. Someone could have climbed the eight- foot chain-link fence. . . . No, that didn't make much sense. Graham was no more than sixty yards from the clubhouse, in full view of the pro shop windows; a ridiculously public place for a murder, even with the fog beginning to drift in as it had the previous evening.

On the other hand, that applied to insiders too. No murderer would pick a spot like this—which suggested that it hadn't been *picked* at all; that it had been a spur-of-the-moment, unpremeditated act. A crime of passion? Sudden, overwhelming anger? Whatever, the killer had been outrageously lucky not to have been seen.

Paul Davis, the Salinas lab's chief criminalist, was still inside the tent, hunched on his knees next to the body. When he saw Graham he got to his feet with a grimace and pressed both hands against the small of his back.

"My oh my, I've been on my knees for an hour. I'm getting too old for this."

Graham looked down at the gray-white corpse made more pathetic rather than less by the cheerful orange-and-yellow golf outfit. Just when was it you were supposed to be young enough for this?

"Enjoying the peace and quiet of small-town law enforcement?" Davis asked with a grin. He stripped off his throw-away plastic gloves, poured two cardboard cups of coffee, and handed Graham one. They had met seven years before in Oakland, when Graham had been only the second cop in the patrol division to have an M.A. and Paul had just become the first black supervising criminalist and the first Ph.D. in the department. Oddballs both, they had become friends.

"You know," Graham said, "this is only the second murder they've had here in six years. I just happened to arrive at the wrong time. Or maybe the right time. What do you have?"

"Well, there's a lot of lab work to be done, and until there's an autopsy I wouldn't want to say for sure—"

"Same old Paul," Graham said, shaking his head. "Hedging your bets all the way. I guess that's the way you get to be a chief criminalist."

Paul laughed. "All right, for you I'll make an exception, just so long as you understand it's not official."

"Understood."

"Okay." They walked a few steps to look more directly down at Kate's body. "Cause of death would seem to be a depressed fracture of the left parietal, resulting in at least two massive bone fragments rupturing the dura mater."

"She would have died immediately?"

"No, not necessarily, but she'd have lost consciousness. The actual cause of death might be drowning, if that's what you mean, but we'll find that out at the lab. I can't see that it makes much difference."

"Neither can I," Graham said. "What can you tell me about the murder weapon?"

"Not much at this point. About all I can say is it seems to have been—"

"Don't tell me. A blunt instrument."

"You got it. A rock, maybe. There were some in the lake."

"Single blow?"

"Single blow. No other injuries. Doc Lefebvre went over her pretty thoroughly."

"Any signs of sexual tampering?"

"No, nothing. Just the one blow to the head. Come on over here, Graham." He walked four or five steps to a roped-off patch of grass about ten feet from the pond. "This is where it happened. "There was blood and a little brain tissue on the grass, and you can see where she fell."

"I can?"

"Well, maybe not *you*, but an expert and perceptive observer such as myself. Then she was dragged to the water and dumped in."

"Any footprints?"

"I'm afraid not. As you can see, the grass goes right up to the water's edge, and the ground is baked hard. Over a week without rain."

Graham took his first sip of the coffee and grimaced. "I see you still like your coffee on the strong side."

"With these cups, if you don't make it strong it tastes like cardboard."

"I think that might be an improvement. Paul, I'm getting the feeling you're not coming up with too much."

"Oh, I don't know. We have a lot of lab work to do yet. We took some earth samples for spectrographic analysis, we did a sweep search of the whole area, including the tee, we dragged the pond—oh, we turned up something interesting in there."

He led Graham back to the others. Graham took advantage of the opportunity to put down his nearly full cup.

"This," Paul said, gesturing at a sodden Wilson golf bag of red-and-white leather, with about a dozen clubs in it. K. O'BRIAN was stenciled on the leather in cracked white paint just above the pouch. "I figure the killer threw it in after her, trying to keep the murder hidden as long as possible."

Graham nodded. "That makes sense. With the bag gone like that, it could have been days before anybody realized anything had happened to her."

"It *would* have been days. The body wouldn't have floated up until maybe the end of the week. We've been pretty lucky here, Graham."

"You're telling me. Paul, is there a chance one of those clubs could be the murder weapon?"

"Could be. We'll make a cast of the wound depression and try matching it to the club heads. Just from a quick look,

I'd say the driver, the three-wood, and the four-wood are distinct possibilities. Maybe even the wedge or the nine-iron, depending on the angle of contact. Not the long irons though, or—"

"Paul," Graham said with some irritation, "if that's supposed to be English—"

Paul's eyebrows slid slowly up. "You mean you don't know how to play golf? How are you going to get through this case?"

"What's that got to do with it? If it was a circus performer who got killed, would I have to know how to swing on a trapeze? If it was a rabbi, would I have to convert?" It sounded good, but Graham wasn't so sure he was convincing himself. "Look, forget what I know or don't know about golf. Would the kind of evidence you're talking about be admissible in court? Matching a cast of a wound to a club?"

"Would it be admissible? Sure. Would it stand up? That depends on who your expert witness is." He grinned. "In this case, have no fear. But we'll do more than make casts. We'll go over every club for blood, hair, skin tissue—"

"After twenty hours underwater?"

"Science," said Paul, tapping the side of his head with a slender, dark forefinger, "is replete with wonders."

"So why," Graham asked, "do I have this rotten feeling that I'm in for one hell of a lot of nasty, old-fashioned, non-scientific legwork?"

4

TO HER SURPRISE Lee slept soundly and awakened in a calm if melancholy frame of mind. There was, after all, nothing she could do about Kate's death (she still found it hard to say "murder," even to herself), and Lieutenant Sheldon had a steady, resolute way about him that suggested the investigation was in good hands. Now, with the air fresh and fragrant, and the early-morning sunlight slanting through the angular pine trees, and a lovely, patchy, pearly mist hugging the fairways of Spyglass Hill, she was feeling as close to cheerful as the situation allowed.

An hour earlier she'd been startled to find her own face smiling out at her from the San Francisco *Post* under a headline that said "Grim Practice Session for Rising Young Star." Some reporter had gotten hold of one of her publicity photos and devoted two columns to speculating on the probable effects of the "deeply traumatic experience" on her career and her psyche.

"Only time will tell" had been the profound conclusion. The remainder of the article was equally insightful; not surprising, since the reporter hadn't even gone to the trouble of getting in touch with her. Her first reactions had been embarrassment and annoyance, but of course by tomorrow—well, by next week—it would be old news and forgotten. Or so she hoped.

And she had appreciated the "rising young star."

She'd splurged and treated herself to a sustaining breakfast of bacon and eggs at the Spyglass Grill, and that had been a big help in filling up the sick, hollow feeling she'd been carrying around since the day before, even if it had demolished her remaining breakfast budget for the tournament.

She was optimistic too. So far, her pre-play practice was going well, and although some golfers looked on that as a bad-luck sign, Lee didn't. She had started with her nine-irons, the shortest-driving, most lofted of the regular clubs, and lobbed a dozen balls to within two or three yards of where she wanted them, fifteen feet beyond the hundred-yard marker. Then she had gradually increased her distance in the usual way, practicing with alternate irons: the seven, the five, the three, and then the woods, until she was sailing the ball well over two hundred arrow-straight yards, her rhythm easy and consistent. It was her standard pregame routine.

Well, not quite. She'd cheated a little. When she'd come to the three-wood she'd vacillated, her hand on the club head. Sometimes the intangibles like morale and the state of mind were more important than the technicalities, and her attitude about the day's play was increasingly positive, so why spoil a good thing? If she hadn't figured out what she was doing wrong with the three-wood in half an hour's work the night before, she wasn't going to do it now, with only fifteen minutes to their 7:30 A.M. starting time. Her best bet was just to stay away from it during the tournament, using the four-wood or the two-iron in its place and adjusting her swing accordingly.

Later, when she had a chance for a coaching session with Cobe, he'd probably take one look and tell her what she was doing wrong, and that would be the end of that. Like the time she'd suddenly lost her touch with the driver for no reason she could think of, and he had told her after watching just two swings that she'd begun underrotating her hips so that she wasn't getting her legs into it. And he'd been right too. Just as he'd been right about her temporary but maddening difficulties with the wedge and the putter. Let's hope the problem was equally simple this time.

There was just time to clean her clubs, which she'd understandably forgotten to do the day before, and she lugged her bag to a nearby bench and began going over them with the toothbrushlike gadget she used for the job.

Wilma Snell, who was taking Kate's place in the tournament, was doing the same thing a few feet away. Wilma was one of the sadder figures on the tour, a muscular woman of forty who looked five years older and was visibly losing whatever ability she'd once had. She had been at it almost twenty years, since the start of the WPGL, and while her plodding style of play had never made her a star or brought her even close to winning a major tournament, she had been among the top ninety on the money list for most of those years. True, never higher than thirty-fifth, but within that magic circle of ninety.

At least it seemed magical to Lee, currently in the hundred thirty-ninth spot according to this week's ratings. It wasn't that being number ninety in women's golf meant a decent income, equal to a secretary's or a schoolteacher's, for example (it didn't). What it did was give you exempt status for the following season; a whole glorious year of automatic eligibility for every one of the thirty-six WPGL tournaments, and who could tell what that might mean? No more Monday qualifying rounds competing against the other hungry rabbits for whatever spaces were left; no more playing your way to unfamiliar towns only to have a bad Monday and wind up deeper in debt than ever, with nothing to do for a week except eat up more of your expense money.

Wilma had been going downhill for the last few years, slipping lower and lower, from forty-sixth, to eightieth, to ninety-first, where she'd come in the past year, just sixty-three dollars behind number ninety. As a result, this year she'd had to fight to qualify with the rest of them, tournament by tournament, for the first time since her rookie season. And like the rest of them, she'd frequently failed to make it. She was now hovering somewhere around ninety-first or ninety-second, and with only a few weeks of the official season left, this was a huge break for her—a possibility of getting a jump on her competitors and making it back into the magic circle.

Lee had always been a little uncomfortable around her. Older rabbits often made young rabbits nervous. Were they a sign of what was to come? Year after sleazy year of watching one's never-more-than-mediocre talent fade away while every season brought another surge of repulsively young, energetic players fresh out of the tour-qualifying school, every one of them unrestrainedly eager to elbow you even farther down the money list?

At this moment the thought of contact with Wilma was particularly unappealing. With an 86 she had missed the cut by a single stroke. It had taken Kate's murder to get her into the tournament, and the thought of this dreary woman—or anyone—benefiting from that was horrible.

But that was small-minded and ridiculous, and Lee knew it. It was tough enough on Wilma without being cold-shouldered by a snotty kid not much more than half her age.

"Hi there, Wilma," she said brightly. "Good luck today."

"Yeah, thanks," Wilma said without looking up, but only a shade more glumly than usual. "Some way to get into a tournament."

"Well, it's certainly not your fault," Lee said, feeling magnanimous.

"No, it's not my fault." Abruptly she stood up and shouldered her bag. "Good luck to you too," she said stiffly, apparently as an afterthought, and headed off.

Lee had the impression that she hadn't really been ready to go yet. Did it work both ways then? Did young rabbits make old rabbits uncomfortable? Probably so, and with more reason. What a way to make a living.

She had finished cleaning her irons and was about to start on the woods when an agitated Peg spotted her.

"Where have you been? We only have two minutes before we tee off. Let's *go*!"

"You're kidding!" But a glance at her watch confirmed it. She looked uneasily at her clubs. "Oh, dear."

"What's the problem. How dirty can they be? There hasn't been any rain for days."

"I know," Lee said, hefting her bag onto her shoulder. "but Lou is going to give me hell for it anyway."

Peg eyed her quizzically. "I don't think you're supposed to be afraid of your caddie. Besides, you're bigger than he is."

"I know, it's just that—well, he's twice as old as I am, and he takes everything so . . . seriously."

He was waiting for her, gnarled and impatient, near the starter's table, and he took it seriously. He looked at Lee, then at her clubs, then at Lee again, all equally reproachfully. "You got enough troubles without starting off with dirty clubs," he muttered darkly, and hoisted the bag's strap onto his own sturdy shoulder. "Tonight *I'll* take care of them."

The "you" was not a happy sign. If he'd been anticipating a good day it would have been "we." It was a common trait with caddies. Like most other pros, Lee could always count on someone with whom to share her triumphs, minor though they might be. But she suffered her defeats alone.

"Sorry," she said firmly, determined to stand up to him, "but I never got a chance to clean them last night after my practice session. You must have heard about Kate O'Brian."

The lines on Lou's seamed face settled in more deeply. "Yeah, I heard," he said. He pulled the towel from around his neck and began rubbing at the club heads without much effect. "What a bummer."

That it was, Lee thought, only he didn't know the half of it. They walked together to the starter's table to join Peg and the other two women in her foursome. There wasn't much of a crowd on hand; most of the spectators wouldn't begin arriving until ten-thirty or eleven, when the better-known players appeared for their tee-off times. Nevertheless, there were fifteen or twenty early birds watching from behind the yellow rope barrier that surrounded the first tee on three sides.

"Oh, look," she heard a woman say, her voice carrying well on the moist air. "There's Lee Ofsted."

Lee brightened. Someone who'd read about her sharp play of three under par on the first round of the Los Angeles

Classic a couple of weeks before? That had been a great round. She'd been in seventh place at the end of the first day.

And thirty-seventh at the end of the fourth.

"Which one?" a bored male voice responded, then grew more interested. "The one with the legs? In the teeny little skirt?"

"You're public," Peg said to Lee out of the side of her mouth. "Ain't they wunnerful?"

"Those are culottes, Floyd," the woman replied coldly. "And I don't see anything special about her legs."

The man reserved his thoughts on this to himself, and Lee was uncomfortably conscious of being silently scrutinized, but after a second he said, "So who's Lee Ofsted?"

She couldn't help trying to hear the answer while she did some final stretching to loosen her back muscles, but it was whispered too quietly. Floyd's reply, however, was all too audible.

"You're kidding," he said reverently. "The one who actually dragged the body out of the water?"

Lee sighed. The pleasures of fame. Thank you, *San Francisco Post*.

The starter tapped the microphone to test it before announcing them, and Lee worked to clear her mind. If she shot no worse than par today, they'd almost certainly make the second-day cut for Saturday's final pro-am round. More important, Lee would be back in the running for Sunday's pros-only round for the big money.

Sara Tollefson, or maybe it was Linda Morton—Lee couldn't keep the two straight, possibly because they both had horsey, long-nosed faces, or maybe because they were both married to orthodontists—hooked her drive into the woods; the other sent hers into the right rough; and Peg's plopped into a fairway bunker. But Lee drove her ball powerfully down the left side, just where she wanted it, and they strode off down the first green fairway of Spyglass Hill.

Spyglass Hill. With its name out of *Treasure Island* (Robert Louis Stevenson had lived for a while in nearby Monterey), Spyglass was possibly the prettiest course in California, probably the best engineered, and certainly the toughest. Despite the dreadful practice of giving the holes names—Billy Bones, Skeleton Island, the Black Spot—so that you sometimes felt you were on a miniature golf course with waterwheels and dragons and Astroturf—it was magnificent. Up, down, and around the great, sloping hill it wound, through pine groves and dunes, with spectacular, distracting views of ocean, beach, and rocky coves. It was a thinking player's course, unusual in that it provided opportunities, not always welcome, to use every one of the fourteen clubs that a golfer is allowed to carry.

It was more of a thrill for her to play on this hallowed ground than she'd have been willing to admit to the others, even to Peg. Did they guess that she'd never been on it before this week? She doubted it. To her three partners, Spyglass was old hat; they had each played it many times. That's what came, she supposed sourly, of choosing an intelligent career like marrying an orthodontist, or of running your own highly successful management consulting firm, the way Peg did. But with daily green fees of sixty dollars, Lee was unlikely to become a habitué any time soon. The only way she was going to get on it again in the foreseeable future was the way she'd done it this time: scrambling her way in as a tournament competitor. No charge that way.

The early holes, constructed over sandy dunes, were notoriously difficult, exposed to the unpredictable weather lashing in from the Pacific. But today the sun shone, the ocean was calm, and the infamous wind held back. Her partners gradually lost their starting jitters, and Lee's game was at its best, with two birdies and three pars after five holes.

Even Lou was pleased, although you had to know him to tell. When her play was poor he usually turned dour and uncommunicative, brooding over some deep and painful problem (such as the probable size of his 5 percent share of her prize money). And whenever she played *terribly*, he became chirpy and loquacious, full of well-meant but misplaced optimism, the way he'd been yesterday.

But when she was good, he turned into the caddie every golfer dreamed of: unobtrusive, supportive, always ready with information on yardage or solid advice on strategy. And that's the way he was today, anticipating her needs, having the right club halfway out of the bag before she asked for it.

It wasn't until her second stroke on the par-five seventh hole, Indian Village, that she made her first bad shot of the day. She watched with a sinking heart as a straightforward 200-yarder sliced badly and ripped into the larger of two sand traps to the right of the green. There went her hopes for another birdie. She'd be lucky to make par on this one; more likely she'd bogey it. Damn.

As she stared miserably after the ball Lou took the offending club from her hand. "Maybe I ought to just bury this goddamn three-wood," he grumbled to himself.

Lee turned abruptly toward him. "You gave me the three?"

"Sure."

"Why?" she snapped. "I don't remember asking for it."

"You didn't ask for anything," he shot back. "You were looking at the green, all dreamy, and you stuck your hand out, and I put it in it." He was clearly offended. "It was the right club. First time you needed it. Hundred ninety-five to the edge of the green, two ten to the pin. If you used the four—" He stopped, aware that she wasn't listening.

"Lou," she said slowly, "how did my swing seem to you?"

He shrugged. "Fine. Perfect."

"I mean just now, specifically; the last shot."

"Perfect," he said again, watching her closely, his head cocked. "What's going on?"

"I'm an idiot," she said, her excitement rising. "Why didn't I think of it before? If my swing is perfect, the shot should be perfect, right?"

"Well—"

"Of course it should. A club-swinging machine can hit perfect balls all day long because its dynamics are mathematically perfect. And there's no wind today, so it can't be that."

"Yeah, I suppose so," he said uncomfortably. Theoretical discussions were not his forte. "Hey, we better get going,

Lee. We're holding up the action, and a two-stroke penalty we don't need."

They walked down the fairway toward the green together, Lee silent and ruminating. At the edge of the bunker they stopped and waited. The other three were all farther back and would shoot first.

Lou pulled out the sand wedge. "You're going to have to explode out," he said. "You're only a couple of yards from the edge, and that lip—"

But again she wasn't listening. "Lou, let me have that three-wood."

His jaw dropped. "The *three*—"

"Just to look at," she said soothingly. "I haven't gone crazy."

He looked as if he weren't so sure, but he put away the wedge and got the wood out again.

"If it's not my swing," she explained, "then it has to be the club. Something must be wrong with it. Or at least something *could* be wrong with it."

"I guess so, but, you know, I'm just a caddie," he said with improbable modesty. "Maybe there's something wrong with your swing and I just can't tell."

"Maybe." Lee took the club and examined it carefully with her eyes and hands. "Well, the shaft's straight, and the flex feels right." She twisted it at its base. "The hosel's tight. . . ." Was she wrong then? Was it her swing after all? She closed one eye and drew an imaginary line down the front of the shaft and along the bottom edge of the club face.

"So can we get going?" Lou said impatiently.

"Wait a minute!" Suddenly agitated and confused, she pulled the other woods out of the bag and looked closely at them, then stared at the three-wood again.

"Lou, this isn't my club. The angle of the club face is different. It's been altered—"

"Maybe you bent it."

"No," she maintained. "Professionally altered. Look, the face has been shaved to change the alignment. How could that be? How—"

But she knew how it could be. Some deep, self-protective

part of her mind tried to block out the flicker of memory, but she remembered all the same. She remembered the first time she'd really talked with Kate. . . .

Having had a miserable final round at Bent Tree in June, Lee had been sitting in front of her locker, glumly gathering up her things, getting ready to move on to the next tournament, when Kate came in, fresh from a round of 67.

She pulled off her white, sweaty visor, rubbed her forehead with the back of her hand, and dropped down on the bench with an angry grunt.

"That damn Kendall," she muttered. "What a miserable temper. As if I did it on purpose."

Kate seemed to notice her for the first time. Her frown disappeared, to be replaced by a smile. "Hey, you really bopped some beauts today. You had nothing but tough luck out there, kid. Too bad."

Normally Lee might have bristled at the "kid," but not from Kate O'Brian, and not for that matter from anyone else in her eighteenth year on the tour.

Lee smiled back. "Next time." She was astonished that someone like Kate would even be aware of her.

"You know, I was watching your swing today, Lee, and it's not that different from mine."

Lee was thrilled. "It's no accident about the swing, Kate. I can remember watching you on television when I was a little girl and—" She flushed, aware that what she'd meant as a compliment had gone a little awry.

But Kate only threw back her head and laughed. "Well, at least you modeled yourself after the best. Look, what I'm getting at is this: I've got a new set of clubs waiting for me, and I thought you might be interested in having the ones I've been using. They're still in good shape, and they'd probably be just right for you."

"I'm sure you're right, but I don't think I could afford—that is, I'm a little short right now—"

Kate laughed again. "I don't want to sell them to you, honey, I want to give them to you. If you want them."

"Give them to me!" Lee knew full well that Kate's Sawyer Featherlites were among the most expensive clubs made, costing at least a thousand dollars more than her own decent but worn Walter Hagens.

"It's no big deal," Kate answered. "That hook I've picked up is chronic, so I finally gave up on correcting it and took the easy way out. I ordered some new ones, same model, and had the woods adjusted for it. So now I can't use the old ones."

But it was a big deal, if not to Kate, then to Lee. True, the six or eight hundred dollars her old clubs could have brought might not mean very much to Kate O'Brian, but all she would have had to do to get it was to tell her caddie to pass the word—and surely nobody ever got rich enough to feel that a single spoken sentence was too much bother for that money. No, in effect, Kate's friendly offer to Lee was six or eight hundred dollars out of her own pocket.

But it wasn't simply that which moved Lee. She had been on the tour over three months, rubbing shoulders with the great names of the game, and never before had one of the established stars gone beyond vacant politeness to genuine friendliness. For the first time, there in the locker room, she had begun to feel that she was something more than an intruder from the wrong side of the tracks who had inexplicably been let into an otherwise exclusive and homogeneous club.

Possibly it was because Kate had come from the wrong side of the tracks herself and felt sympathy for a kindred spirit. In any case, Lee had gratefully accepted the clubs (and been able to sell her own for two hundred much-needed dollars), and she and Kate had become friends of a sort, although the differences in age, status, and lifestyle had never let them become very close.

And now, standing at the edge of a sand trap on Spyglass Hill, looking down at the club in her hands, she had finally figured out what she should have realized hours before. A hook is a curving of the ball to the left. When a club head's angle is adjusted to correct it, what it does is introduce a curve to the right that compensates for the hook and, in effect, straightens it out. And what happens when a player who doesn't have a hook hits a golf ball with a club that has been so adjusted? Obviously, the ball curves to the right instead of going straight.

And a ball that curves to the right instead of going straight is known as a slice.

It was Kate's new three-wood in her hand; somehow, in some unexplainable way, it had found its way into her bag with Lee's clubs. She frowned down at it. How could that be? What had happened to her own three-wood? Had they inadvertently switched clubs on the practice tee Wednesday evening, the night Kate was killed? It couldn't have been before then, because she hadn't started slicing until Thursday's round. And it couldn't have been after, because . . . well, because Kate was dead, and her clubs were in the lake with her. But how *could* they have switched . . .

"Lee?" It was Lou, holding out the sand wedge to her. "Come on, the marshal's coming over." He reached out to take the three-wood from her hand.

But Lee shook her head, staring at the club, a nibbling apprehension crawling across her scalp and down her neck. That hideous, craterlike pit in Kate's pale temple, under the wet, slimy hair . . .

"Miss Ofsted?" A marshal approached her hesitantly. "Would you mind continuing, please? We're running a little behind."

Again Lee shook her head, hardly hearing her. She forced herself to look even more closely at the club face. The scoring lines—horizontal, parallel grooves inscribed in the metal face plate to provide friction—had bits of grass and black earth embedded in them from yesterday's play. Nothing surprising about that. But the top two grooves, which should have been cleaner than the rest, weren't. The were lined with a brown, caked substance. And there was more of it in the thin crevice between hosel and shaft. Grimacing, she scraped gingerly at it with her thumbnail, praying it would crumble just like any other dirt.

It didn't. It flaked. Just like dried blood.

Summoned by the scorer's walkie-talkie, the security force of the Pacific-Western Pro-Am arrived in the form of a middle-aged, round-bellied man in a green uniform who drove up in a white Yamaha golf cart. "Security" said the cardboard placard stuck with Scotch tape to the upper right corner of the window. Watching him climb importantly from the cart, Lee had the impression he would have had a red flashing light on the roof if he could have gotten away with it, and maybe a siren as well.

"All right, now," he said in a nasal and excited voice, "everybody just relax. I'm Officer Quimby. Do I understand that you believe this to be the weapon in question in the homicide case now under investigation?"

"I'm not sure," Lee said. "But I thought I'd better call you." Inappropriate as it was, there was a bubble of laughter at the base of her throat. She wondered disrespectfully if Officer Quimby spent his off-duty hours studying Don Knotts on reruns of the old "Andy Griffith Show."

She held the club out to him and with a flourish he whipped out a handkerchief to grasp it by the shaft, then propped it handle side down, against the cart's passenger seat. If the purpose of the handkerchief was to preserve fingerprints, she could tell him right now whose were going to be on them. Hers. Hundreds of them.

With Peg and Lou pressed into service as witnesses, Officer Quimby meticulously noted the date, time, and place on a tag and tied it to the three-wood.

"I'm afraid," he intoned, "that I'll have to take the rest of your clubs too, ma'am." He produced another of his clean white tags from somewhere and licked the point of his pencil.

"But you can't!" Lee exclaimed when his words had sunk in. She wasn't laughing anymore.

Security Officer Quimby's eyebrows rose.

"I mean," she said with more restraint, "not now, at least; not in the middle of the round."

"We have a murder investigation going on here, ma'am," Officer Quimby said in a voice that must have carried to the spectators watching avidly from behind the rope restraints twenty yards away. "I'm not going to take the responsibility of allowing you to continue to play with what may turn out to be material evidence."

"Then suppose you get on the horn to somebody who can," Peg contributed in her forthright manner. "She can't play without her clubs."

"Suppose," Officer Quimby said with narrowed eyes, "that we just wait for Carmel PD to get here and see what they say."

"I'm awfully sorry," a nervous, blue-jacketed marshal put in hesitantly, "but I'm afraid we can't wait any longer. Play is already backed up to the sixth tee."

"I'm sorry, but we have a murder investigation going on here, ma'am—"

"Goddamnit," exploded Lou, who had restrained himself until now, "what are we supposed to do? I mean, we're trying to make a living here, pal."

Officer Quimby, whose size did not allow him to look down at many people, was able to look down at Lou, and this he did, with a pronounced scowl that Lou, a world-class scowler, returned with interest. Fortunately, before this could escalate, Sergeant Rubio and a uniformed policeman were driven up in two more golf carts.

Lee was not overly pleased to see the nervous sergeant whose anxious mothering the day before had done little to settle her down. But this morning he seemed firmly in control. In less than two minutes he and a respectful Officer Quimby had left in one of the carts with their material evidence and Lee was allowed to proceed, with the policeman following her at a discreet distance to make sure that she didn't do whatever they were afraid she might do with the rest of her clubs. What she did, surprisingly enough, was to shoot a respectable 71.

Graham Sheldon was leaning against a tree, waiting for her, when they holed out at the eighteenth green a little less than three hours later. It took her a moment to recognize him, since he wasn't wearing a sports coat and tie as he had the day before, but casual slacks, a knit shirt, and a green windbreaker that made him look like one of the spectators.

"Uh-oh, looks like someone wants to talk to me," she

said to Peg as they left the scoring tent. "An autograph seeker, no doubt."

"No doubt," Peg said. "Chin up, sweetie. See you later."

"Thanks for letting me finish," Lee said to him while she nervously watched Lou grudgingly hand her clubs to the policeman, who left to take them to the lab. "Can I get them back by tomorrow?"

"Oh, I think so." He smiled a greeting. "How did it go out there?"

She stripped off her glove and tucked it into a side pocket. "All things considered, amazingly well. It looks as if our team's going to make the cut."

"The cut?"

She looked at him, astonished. "You don't know what a cut is?"

He looked back at her and smiled. "Am I supposed to?"

"You darn well are," she almost said. How could he possibly handle a case like this if he didn't even know that much about golf?

But she thought she'd be better off keeping her reservations to herself. "The cut," she explained, "is the dividing line between the people who get to play in the final rounds and the ones who don't. In the Pacific-Western, if your team is still in the top half of the field after Friday, your group can compete in the last round of the pro-am on Saturday. Every pro who gets to play is guaranteed three hundred dollars for starters."

She hesitated, then decided there was no reason to try to impress him. "I can use the money, Lieutenant."

"I know," he said noncommittally. He glanced at the crowd bustling about them. "Look, how about finding someplace where we can have a private talk?"

"Do I have a choice?"

"Nope, afraid not." He steered her firmly by the elbow to a wooded rise out of sight of the green and behind one of the yellow-and-white striped hot dog tents. They both sat cross-legged on the cool grass. Graham leaned back against a pine tree and looked expectantly at her.

Lee stirred uncomfortably. Was he hoping for a full confession from her, or what? She had noticed yesterday that he had a way of looking at her that made her feel like a beetle pinned to a bug collection card, and a guilty beetle at that. No doubt it came in handy when dealing with recalcitrant criminals. But she wasn't being recalcitrant, and she certainly wasn't a criminal. She returned his stare as firmly as she could, which wasn't too firmly. But this wasn't his beetle-pinning glower, she realized belatedly; not quite your down-home, neighborly gaze either, but a look of—what? Reserve? Distance? Evaluation?

"All right," he said easily, "I'll start. I just thought there might be a pertinent question you wanted to ask first."

She grasped instantly what he meant. "The club—was it the—is that what killed Kate?"

"Yes." He waited a moment, as if allowing it to sink in. "I don't suppose you'd care to speculate on how she came to be killed with one of your clubs?"

"*My* club? That isn't my club, it was *hers*!"

He seemed genuinely surprised. "Those aren't your clubs?"

"Yes. I mean no. I mean, all of them are mine except that one, the three-wood. Somebody must have taken mine out of my bag and substituted hers instead. I know it sounds farfetched, but—" Only there weren't any buts. Nervously she stopped in midsentence and waited for him to say something.

"And just how could that happen?" he asked after a long, cool silence.

Lee was suddenly frightened. He didn't believe her. Surely he couldn't possibly think she'd killed Kate. Or maybe not so surely.

She shook her head. "I don't know; I've been thinking about it all through the round. The only thing I can come up with is that if Kate really was killed during the time I was back at the clubhouse—"

"She was."

"—then the murderer must have put it there accidentally."

"Come again?"

"Well, when I went in for the tea, I left my bag next to

hers in the bag rack, and when I came back out she was gone. My bag was still sitting there."

"You just left it out on the practice tee? Why didn't you take it into the clubhouse with you?"

"Why should I do that?"

"I thought they were worth a lot of money."

"They are. More than I could afford, as a matter of fact. But Kate was right there, and I was only going to be gone for a few minutes."

"Then why weren't you more surprised when you got back and saw that she'd taken off and just left them there?"

"Well, I hadn't actually *asked* her to keep an eye on them, you know." She picked anxiously at the grass near her ankles. It was definitely bug-pinning time again. "Anyway, my name is painted on the bag in big white letters, and the area was closed to the public, and—well, it's just not the sort of thing you worry about at a place like Carmel Point."

"I see," he said dryly.

"Nobody *did* steal the bag, you know."

"No," he said with the ghost of a smile, "nobody stole the bag." He shifted and stretched out his legs, crossing them at the ankles. It was impossible to read his expression. "Let's go back to the club itself. What makes you think it's hers and not yours?" Before she could answer he added: "They look like a set to me, including that three-wood. To my sergeant and the criminalists too. Same make—Sawyer Featherlites—same green-and-white hand-grips, same model number on all the shafts: S358."

"Well, sure. That's because 'my' clubs are actually Kate's old oncs. She gave them to me when she got new ones, and the sets are identical. Don't you have her set too? If you compare them you'll see."

"I'll do that. But if they're identical, what makes you so sure that was hers in your bag?"

But she could see he was beginning to believe her. She hadn't realized the muscles at the back of her neck had bunched, but now she felt them relax a little. "Kate's new set—the one she's been using since she gave me the old ones—was adjusted for her hook. So when I finally got smart enough to take a good, hard look at that three-wood after slicing for two days, and I saw that the face had been opened up to compensate for a hook, I knew it had to be hers. I also knew where that slice of mine came from."

When he continued to look blankly at her after she'd finished this lucid if slightly jittery explanation, she said, "Uh, did you want me to go through that again?"

He leaned forward. "The part about hooks and slices and compensations, if you don't mind. With annotations."

The disturbing notion that Graham Sheldon didn't know what the hell he was doing loomed again. She began an elementary lecture on open and closed club faces and the trajectories they created, but he grasped the essentials before she finished her third sentence, and she told herself that it would pay to remember that he was not unintelligent but merely ignorant.

He settled back against the tree trunk. Lee wished she'd had the good sense to sit down against a tree too. She'd had a long morning's golf, and her back was beginning to ache. She considered moving the couple of feet necessary to brace herself against a tree but decided he might regard it as evidence of guilty anxiety. She stayed where she was.

"I wonder where your *own* three-wood is," he said slowly, looking at her again with that odd, reflective quality, as if he couldn't make up his mind about something. It was a big improvement over the beetle-impaling glower.

She tried a smile. "Something tells me you already know."

He laughed, not unkindly. "I think I just figured it out."

"Did someone find it near the tee box?" she asked.

He shook his head and looked soberly at her. "This is just a guess, but according to the report there aren't any clubs missing from Kate's bag. It was listed as a complete set. That would include a three-wood, wouldn't it?"

She nodded.

"Okay," he said, "then if you were playing with *her* three-wood I've got to assume that the one in her bag—"

"Was mine?" Lee said dully. "In Kate's bag? But that doesn't make any sense."

"You couldn't have put it there accidentally?"

Lee shook her head crisply. "Of course not. No more than you could accidentally drive your car into someone else's garage. And no one else did it accidentally either. When I went in for tea I didn't leave any clubs lying around. I put them all in my own bag; I always do."

"Look, do you suppose you could come into the station later this afternoon and see if you can identify it?"

"I think so. It's got a nick in the heel, and of course it won't have been adjusted, and—and . . ." She faltered as the significance of what she'd been told finally sank in. "Now wait a minute. There's no way this could have happened accidentally. Somebody had to do it on purpose. I mean, someone went to the trouble of taking my club out of my bag and putting it in Kate's, and taking Kate's club out of her bag and putting it in mine." She stared confusedly at him.

"Looks like it."

"And it must have been done after she was killed. Otherwise there wouldn't have been any blood on the club."

He nodded approvingly.

"But—but why? What would have been the point?" But the answer was too obvious to miss and, reluctantly, she supplied it herself. "You were *supposed* to believe that was my wood with the blood on it. Someone's tried to make it look as if *I* did it."

"That's one possibility. Another possibility," he said pleasantly, "is that you actually did do it, and then got confused in the heat of the moment."

She looked at him levelly, emitting what she hoped was wry amusement, 80 percent sure that he hadn't meant it. The other 20 percent of her was quaking in its socks. Who could tell, maybe this was some kind of police technique to throw murderers off their stride.

"I hope you're not serious," she said with a relaxed and confident smile. And quiveringly held her breath while he appraised her with another of those long, cool, evaluative looks.

"How about a hot dog?" he asked unexpectedly. "I'll buy."

She expelled the breath with a laugh. "Well, I'll say this,

Lieutenant: It's the first time I've been accused of murder in one sentence and offered a hot dog in the next."

He rose to his feet and held out his hand for her to take, but she got up on her own.

"Look, Lieutenant—" She hesitated. "You don't really think I killed Kate, do you?"

"Correct. I don't really think you killed Kate." He brushed the grass off his slacks and said without a trace of a smile: "Of course, I've been wrong before."

The turning point had come the moment before he'd mentioned the hot dogs. She had suddenly recognized the strangely troubling gaze with which he'd been fixing her. It was by no means the look with which a detective freezes a suspect (not according to the movies, anyway); it was, in fact, not the kind of look a detective uses at all. Not in his work.

What it was, was a me-man-you-woman look, and the reason she hadn't realized it before was because it was so unexpected. And so unselfconscious. He wasn't trying to overwhelm her with charm or masculinity, both of which he had in ample supply, or to assert the power of his authority over her, or to send her any other message. He was doing what it looked like he was doing: evaluating, thinking, wondering about the possibilities; or perhaps wondering about the propriety of wondering, given the circumstances.

While he stood in line to buy the hot dogs she found a bench and considered additional ramifications of this astonishing new development. It didn't take long to decide how she felt about it: good. What she thought about it was another matter. This was no time in her life for complications; golf took all her energy and most of her hours. On the other hand, who said things had to get complicated? And how often did she meet a genuinely attractive man in the bizarre and transient world she lived in? *Never* was the answer, at least if you were talking about unattached men, although the woods were full enough of sleazeballs.

But Graham Sheldon, she heard herself telling herself with some surprise, was extraordinarily attractive, and not just because of the athlete's build, and the clear blue eyes, and the neat, sandy mustache, although none of that hurt either. What he had that was in much shorter supply was an essential decency, a humanity that had come through even yesterday, when she'd been too shaken and disoriented to think about it.

When he came back there was an awkward constraint that hadn't been there before. He straddled the bench at her side and put down the flimsy cardboard box with four hot dogs and two lemonades in it. In silence they unwrapped the foil around two of the hot dogs, tore open the mustard packets, spread the contents, and had their first bites. What exactly was wrong? Did he realize he'd been sending vibrations without meaning to? Or had he meant to, and was he now having second thoughts? Did he read something new in *her* manner?

My God, it was already complicated and they hadn't done anything yet!

"I think I owe you some straight talk," he said, and for a moment she was afraid things were about to get more complicated still. She should have known better. "The answer to your question," he continued, "is no, I don't think you killed Kate. Period. I shouldn't have joked about it."

"Thank you," she said, equally grave. "I'm glad to hear it." With improved appetite, she continued with her hot dog.

"I'm not saying that I didn't have a few doubts yesterday after we checked you out—"

Lee stopped chewing. "Yesterday? I've been a suspect from the very beginning? Even before the club turned up?"

'Oh, I wouldn't quite say a *suspect*." He took a long sip from his paper cup. "It's just that it pays to do some checking on the person who finds a body. Sometimes it's the same person who put it there."

"But that's crazy. Why would a murderer go out of his way to call attention to himself?"

"Precisely because it seems crazy for a murderer to go out of his way to call attention to himself. Or herself." He shrugged, chewing. "It happens."

"I suppose so. Live and learn. Tell me, what did you find out about me that made you have doubts?"

"Well, we dug around and learned that you're in a pretty deep financial hole. Unless you've got a nest egg stashed away somewhere, it's hard to see how you can make it through the season. Expenses are high on the tour—that's another thing I found out."

"It's always possible, you know," she said coolly, "that I might actually win a major tournament."

"I hope you do," he said warmly. "But until then, you'll be living pretty close to the edge, won't you?"

"And I suppose you also found out that that puts me technically in violation of the WPGL rule on having sufficient funds?"

He lifted his eyebrows. "*Technically* in violation? That's kind of a specious distinction, isn't it? Don't forget, I'm a cop; I like things black and white. Overfastidious distinctions go right over my head."

"You sure don't talk like a cop." She laughed. "Okay, *in* violation, if it makes you happier. The rule's discriminatory anyway. Why shouldn't women pros have as much right as men to starve on the tour? The PGA doesn't have a rule like that. I don't think so, anyway."

"Hey, don't get mad at me, lady, I'm on your side." Smiling, he finished his hot dog and began unwrapping another. "All the same, I think it would be a good idea if you leveled with me."

She looked up sharply. "About what?"

"As I understand it, the rules require you to prove you have enough money of your own or enough backing to get you through the season before they'll let you play. Is that right?"

She nodded, wondering where he was leading.

"Okay," he said, "that means that you had the money when the season started. But according to the dogged research put in by the minions of the law, you don't have it now. The question is: Where did it all go?"

She put down the relish packet she'd torn open for her second hot dog and looked him in the eye. "Lieutenant, am I a suspect, or am I not a suspect?" He calmly returned her stare without speaking, and she dropped her eyes and went on. "Well, it's just that everything's more expensive than I thought it'd be: caddies, tournament fees, transportation—"

"Look," he said sharply, "just because *I* don't think you did it doesn't mean the D.A.'s going to agree. He's not as trusting as I am. Now how about just trusting *me* and telling me the truth?"

She almost laughed. Here was this inarguably resourceful detective lieutenant in charge of a homicide investigation in which she was pretty clearly implicated, no doubt a cunning and devious man who would resort to trickery when it suited his purpose, sitting there and looking at her with those sincere blue eyes and blandly telling her to just go ahead and trust him.

Oddly enough, she did. "Well, the simple truth," she said slowly, "is that I neither wanted to sell pieces of myself—you know, pay a percentage of my earnings to a backer—nor go up to my eyebrows in debt to anybody who'd advance the cash. So I borrowed twelve thousand dollars from the manager of the course where I used to work to demonstrate sufficient funds." She shrugged. "And then I gave half of it back to him."

"Another one of those little technical violations," he murmured with a smile. "It's a good thing for you I'm not in the pay of the Women's Golf Association or whatever you call it."

"Women's Professional Golf League. WPGL." She shrugged. "I thought I'd have won some decent money by now."

"Ah."

He was going to say something else, but she spoke first, feeling that she'd been on the defensive long enough. Time for him to answer some questions.

"What I don't understand is what my financial situation has to do with it. So what if I'm short of money? I didn't stand to gain anything from Kate's death." She smiled soberly. "If anything, I lose. Without those rides my transportation costs are going to go up."

"Some people might think," he said slowly, rotating his

lemonade cup and staring down at the dregs, "that a major endorsement contract would more than make up for that."

"A major—I don't mean to sound dim, but I honestly don't know what you're talking about."

He raised his eyes and regarded her gravely.

"Look," she said, increasingly bewildered, "obviously you think I'm not being truthful, but I give you my word . . ." She jerked her head with frustration. "Anyway, why would anyone want me to endorse their equipment? I've never come within a mile of a big win. Of any win, to be honest."

"True, but you must admit you have a certain cosmetic value."

She laughed uncertainly. "Did I just get a compliment?"

"You'll know it when you get a compliment." He paused, frowning. "I know what you and Milt Sawyer talked about at dinner the night Kate died."

She stared confusedly at him for a moment, then burst out laughing.

"I don't know why," he said, "but somehow I get the feeling you might not be taking this altogether seriously. Did I say something funny?"

"Yes, you did. You have to understand, Milt Sawyer is a joke in the golf world. He throws wads of money around, and he loves to be seen at the track and with celebrities, and he loves talking big, but nobody takes him seriously. Not when it comes to Sawyer Sports Equipment. It's Papa Sawyer who makes the endorsement offers, not Milt."

She paused to sip her lemonade. "Milt was going on about tie-ins and signing me up to do some of the things Kate was doing for them because Kate was getting stale, and on and on. But I'd have been crazy to pay any attention to him. Anyway, I had other things to think about."

"I see."

"And there's something else," she said soberly. "I respect Kate O'Brian. I liked her too. Do you think I'd even consider cutting in on one of her sponsors?"

"No, I don't," he said with prompt and gratifying directness. "But why did you go out to dinner with the guy at all?"

Who wanted to know, the man or the cop? Either way, he deserved an honest answer. "For the meal, to be brutally frank. The Monterey Hilton isn't the kind of place I get to eat in very often."

"And it didn't bother him that you weren't paying any attention to him?"

She laughed. "Milt's not the kind who's offended by minor details like whether you're paying attention. If you've interviewed him, you've noticed he's absolutely contented as long as he's talking."

"He's next on my list. I wanted to talk to you first. Tell me, what 'other things' did you have to think about?"

She looked at him for a while, but his expression showed nothing. "Well, I don't remember exactly, of course, but mostly I was replaying the morning's practice round in my head and trying to work out different approaches to the fifth, ninth, and tenth greens, which I expected to give me a lot of trouble the next day. An accurate prediction, as it turned out."

He considered this, and nodded his acceptance. "All right, thanks." He looked at his watch, then began to gather the debris together.

"Wait, Lieutenant; there's something that's bothering me. You said you haven't talked to Milt yet, didn't you?"

"True."

"So how do you know what we talked about at dinner?"

"Oh, there was someone nearby who happened to overhear it."

She thought a moment. "Nick Pittman? The tournament director? I saw him there when I came in."

"Yes, as a matter of fact; Nick Pittman. Not that I really ought to tell you."

"Why would he go out of his way to tell you that?" she asked with a frown.

"Just doing his civic duty. He also told me you'd been with Kate at the practice tee just before she was killed. Which I already knew, of course."

"Nick did? How would he know that?"

"He said you mentioned it after yesterday's round." He tilted his head. "Didn't you?"

"Yes," she said thoughtfully, "I suppose I did."

"Look, don't get paranoid. Pittman isn't going around telling tales about you. I asked him a lot of direct questions and he gave me a lot of direct answers. That's the way it's supposed to work."

"I know," Lee said with a smile. "All right, where do we go from here?"

"We?"

"You don't think I'm going to sit around doing nothing, do you, while someone out there's trying to pin Kate's murder on me?"

"Yes, I do. Oh, I most certainly do. And it's not 'trying,' it's 'tried.' Past tense."

"I don't see much difference."

"There's plenty. I think you're in this by accident. Your bag happened to be in the wrong place at the wrong time. Whoever killed her was just trying to throw suspicion on someone—anyone—not you in particular. You just got lucky, that's all."

"I don't see what—"

"If you start poking around, you might draw his attention back to you. That could put you in danger."

"Sure, but—"

"Sure, nothing. I have enough problems already. Go play golf."

"With what? You have my clubs."

He grinned. "A point. Look, how about coming by the Carmel Police Station about four-thirty? It's on Junipero, right downtown. You can get them then."

She nodded. He got up and tossed their litter into one of the *Fore Waste* trash containers that dotted the course, and when he returned, Lee stood up too. She was five ten, only about three inches shorter than he was, so she could look him straight in the eyes.

"Lieutenant, with the evidence of that golf club against me, why are you so sure I *didn't* do it?"

"Three reasons. First, if that really isn't your club, then

it's not much in the way of evidence, is it? Quite the opposite, really, since it means someone deliberately tried to frame you. Second, you'd hardly have yelled for the police when you found a bloodstained club in your bag if you'd really killed Kate."

"I don't know; wouldn't I? What if I were using the same logic as the murderer who 'discovers' the body?"

He shook his head. " 'Discovering' the body is crazy but cute. Calling the cops about the club would just be plain crazy."

"Uh-huh. What's the third reason?"

"Intuition," he said. "People I like rarely turn out to be murderers."

It pleased her more than he might have guessed. "Which is more important?" she asked. "The club or the intuition?"

"That, ma'am, is for me to know and you to wonder about." He put his hand on her shoulder lightly and blamelessly. "I want you do to me a favor. Don't hang around foggy, deserted tees any more. I don't think you're in any danger, but just in case. Okay?" He removed his hand. Her shoulder was suddenly cold.

"Okay." She smiled at him. "I promise."

She watched him walk away. Was there more to that pat than a small, friendly gesture of support, or was she inventing fantasies? She brushed the thought away for more immediate concerns. Did her promise to stay away from deserted practice tees mean she couldn't do any pertinent "poking around" at all? She didn't think so.

It was Lieutenant Sheldon's job to solve the crime, and she had no doubt that he would . . . eventually. But, capable as he seemed to be, he was severely handicapped: He didn't know the first thing about golf or golfers. He didn't even understand the damn language. In the meantime, how could she simply do nothing while waiting to see what a less-than-trusting district attorney made of the fact that the murder weapon had turned up in her bag? So far she'd been lucky. For one thing there were Graham Sheldon's intuitions. For another whoever had switched the clubs had—fortunately—been unaware of the adjustments in Kate's woods. My God,

Lee thought, where would she be now if she couldn't prove that the bloodied club was Kate's and not hers? No, she couldn't just leave it to luck.

And aside from all that, there might be something she could do to help the lieutenant along, to throw some light on Kate's death. There were all kinds of questions to be answered, and they were very pertinent indeed.

Just why, for example, had nice, nervous Nick Pittman gone out of his way to place her at the murder scene and to provide the police with a whopping motive to implicate her in Kate's death?

5

THAT WAS A good place to start and a first-rate question. Unfortunately, she would have to wait to pursue it. Nick would be the busiest man in Carmel (or at least the most harried) in the middle of the day's play, and hardly in the mood—let alone coherent enough—to answer her questions. Besides, what precisely were her questions?

In the meantime, she was not about to let the afternoon go by without trying to make at least some progress, so, having showered and changed clothes, she flagged down one of the white Ford vans that shuttled players between the courses and took it to Carmel Point, which was tournament headquarters. She was a long way from having any sort of plan, or even knowing where to begin, but it seemed to make sense to head for the center of the action and hope that inspiration would strike.

From force of habit she went immediately to the place most golfers made for after their day's round—not the bar, as popular legend would have it, but the far side of the clubhouse's rear lawn to watch the scores being posted on the five-foot-high, thirty-foot-long cumulative scoreboard. There were the usual clusters of players watching the self-important WPGL scorers scribble away, Magic Markers squeaking, as the scores came in on their mobile phone headsets. Some of the golfers seemed to be there for the purpose of making witty comments as their competitors' scores were entered. Others watched avidly, nervously licking their lips. That was one way, she supposed, of telling the difference between the solid pros who had it made and the insecure rabbits who were barely surviving. Which reminded her . . .

She searched along the board for her own team's standing and was relieved to see that things had improved. The team was now tied for thirty-second, and Lee herself was in thirtieth place among the pros. Given any kind of luck, it seemed likely they were all going to make the cut after all. So much for making a living. She let her eyes roam down the long list of names on the board, all of whom would have had access to the practice tee the night Kate had been killed. The amateurs, except for her own partners, were unfamiliar to her, but she knew most of the pros, at least well enough to say hello to. Were there any likely murderers among them? She almost laughed aloud. These were sane, responsible women (insofar as taking this game seriously was compatible with sanity), not ravening killers who smashed each other over the head with clubs.

Something Graham Sheldon had said came back to her. The murder, he thought, had been unplanned, the result of a loss of temper, probably regretted a split second after it occurred. That made a difference. And to be honest, as much as she liked Kate, she knew well enough that she had a way of setting others off. In the process of battling her way from an Irish-Catholic Boston slum to golf stardom, Kate had finely honed her competitive instincts—or ruthlessly honed them, depending on who you talked to. And at no point along the way had she tried very hard to soften her edges or curb her tongue. To put it mildly, Kate O'Brian was sometimes untactful. To put it bluntly, she could be an enormous pain in the ass when the mood was upon her.

So . . . with that in mind, was there anybody up there on the board, with a temper of her own, who might have been nursing a grudge against Kate?

As if in answer to her question, the Magic Markers entered another foursome's final scores. First, in the happy red that signified better-than-par results, the best-ball group score of

66. Then, in the dreary blue that meant above-par, the pro's individual score, a dismal 80. For Dorothy Kendall.

Dorothy Kendall. What was it Kate had grumbled that day at Bent Tree? Something about Dorothy's temper . . . ? Lee cursed herself for not remembering, but she'd been too absorbed in her own problems to pay much attention to Kate's mutterings and then too excited about the gift of the clubs to follow up. But hadn't there been some gossip about it afterward? Some sort of scorekeeping flap between the two of them? It was a pretty tenuous place to start, but it was a place.

She wandered to the snack wagon near the pro shop and bought a package of Milk Duds. (They lasted longer than anything else.) No, she couldn't remember exactly what Kate had said, but she remembered quite a lot about Dorothy Kendall, and she leaned thoughtfully against a stone retaining wall, chewing doggedly away at the sticky caramel and putting what she knew in order.

Dorothy was a ten-year tour veteran who was in a class of her own when it came to frustrated golfers. As a teenager she'd won two consecutive USGA Junior Girls Championships, then turned professional and stood the golfing world on its ear with a glittering rookie season, and then a second one that was even better. Maybe not quite up to Nancy Lopez's phenomenal early years, but close; she was the number-five money winner in her second year, and everyone said her fluid, effortless swing would last forever.

But of course it didn't. A few years later, in 1981, the swing was no longer so effortless, and she had dropped to twenty-fourth. Ever since, despite her working on and off with her coaches, her game had gone downhill, as had her disposition. Where she ranked now, Lee had no idea; in the fifties, she thought.

There was something else Lee thought she knew about Dorothy: where to find her about three-quarters of an hour from now, after she'd showered and gotten away from the crowds at Spyglass Hill. Lee popped another Milk Dud into her mouth and ambled off in the proper direction. No harm getting there early.

* * *

Dorothy Kendall narrowed her eyes and arched her thin, penciled eyebrows until they disappeared under the permanent-frizzled, bleached blond bangs. Her vaguely Pekingeselike face was lumpy with irritation. "Just what is it you're trying to do," she snapped, "solve the great crime all by yourself?"

They were sitting in one of the red leather booths of The Cormorant, the new clubhouse's "authentic Olde English pub," complete with oak beams, horse brasses, and imitation leaded windows. Until that moment Lee had thought she'd been doing pretty well. She'd taken a seat from which she could keep an eye on the front door, and when Dorothy stalked in, Lee had turned her most engaging smile on her. Dorothy had not been terrifically responsive, but fortunately the other booths and tables were filled by groups of three and four, and the bar had been taken over by a loud and particularly obnoxious trio of middle-aged Romeos, so she hadn't had much choice. She came over with ill-concealed reluctance and joined Lee.

The early conversation had gone according to the plan Lee had developed while sipping Chablis and munching Milk Duds—not a combination she would repeat. First there was the obligatory discussion of the day's round, then a few innocuous questions on technique respectfully delivered, raw newcomer to established pro. When Dorothy ordered her second Scotch, Lee casually dropped her carefully prepared lead-in.

"I guess you'd known Kate for a long time, hadn't you?"

That's what had brought on the sarcasm, and now Lee floundered for something to say while Dorothy continued to stare icily at her through a haze of smoke from her Virginia Slim.

"Who, me?" Lee finally said with a lame laugh. "Solving it? Not on your life. I guess I was just trying to make sense of things—you know, answer some questions in my own mind."

"Questions?" Dorothy blew more smoke out of pinched

nostrils. "Did Dorothy Kendall happen to kill her, for instance?" She gulped angrily at her Scotch.

This was not at all what Lee had had in mind. "Dorothy, I really didn't mean anything personal," she said with another nervous and unconvincing laugh. "Honestly."

"Honestly," Dorothy mimicked and finished the last half of her drink in two swallows. The empty glass was rapped twice on the table to get the waiter's attention and a third drink was ordered. Lee began to get a little uneasy.

"Exactly what's your theory?" Dorothy asked. "That I was so filled with rage because she robbed me of twelfth place at Bent Tree that I bashed in her skull?"

Lee held her peace.

Dorothy's Scotch came and she slid it to the side to allow her to lean forward, elbows on the table. "Now listen, if I had a driver in my hand at the time I'm not saying what might have happened. But three months later? What for? It's over and done."

"Dorothy, I don't even know what it was that happened between the two of you."

The older woman looked doubtfully at her, but then seemed to take her at her word. She sank back against the leather-covered seat and took a swig of Scotch. "Well, that makes me feel better, anyway. I thought everybody in the world was still talking about it." She looked stonily over Lee's shoulder at the lush eighteenth green and sloping fairway below. "You know what happened to Roberto de Vicenzo in sixty-eight, don't you? Or is that ancient history to you?"

"Oh, no!" Lee murmured. It was ancient history, all right, but it had been drummed into every applicant's head at the WPGL school in Miami as a horrific cautionary tale. De Vicenzo had finished the final round of the grueling 1968 Masters tournament with a 64 for a first-place tie, which meant a playoff.

Or so it should have meant. Unfortunately for de Vicenzo, in the Masters as in other tournaments, playing partners keep score for each other on the official scorecards. When the round is done, the player checks his own card to see that his partner has been accurate and signs it—thereby making it final and absolutely unchangeable. What went wrong in this case was that de Vicenzo's partner, Tommy Aaron, had inadvertently recorded an extra stroke for him, giving him a total of 65 instead of 64. De Vicenzo, in the process of being hurried into a television interview, signed the card without checking it, and that was that. When Aaron realized what he'd done a few seconds later it was too late; the poorer score had to stand. Instead of the tie de Vicenzo had earned and a shot at the $20,000 prize—and the Masters title—he had to settle for a bitter second place.

"Only with me it was worse," Dorothy said with a brittle laugh. "Kate didn't give me a stroke *more*, she gave me a stroke *less*."

"A stroke *less*," Lee said with genuine sympathy. "Oh, dear." When an error results in a lower rather than a higher score, she knew, the rules are more merciless still. The golfer is disqualified. No excuses, no explanations, no appeals.

"Oh, dear," Dorothy echoed mincingly. "My very words when they told me about it in the scoring tent." She laughed without humor, a dry bark. "That honest little mistake cost me twelfth place and sixty-one hundred dollars."

Lee slowly shook her head. It wasn't quite the same thing as losing the Masters title, but it was bad enough. More than bad enough to a golfer on the skids.

"Kate must have felt awful," she said. "Didn't she ever—I mean—"

"Offer to pay it back?" Dorothy snorted. "You college kids really think that's what the game is all about, don't you? Well, let me tell you—" She sucked in a last, thin-lipped drag on the cigarette, then fiercely stubbed it out in the ashtray, grinding it to a brown mess with a brown hand from which the rigid tendons seemed about to burst. "Let me tell you, the money was nothing. But twelfth place was my first decent finish in almost a year and a half. I was on my way again; I could feel it. You get a momentum—" She had throbbed with energy for a moment but now sank back against her seat again, smoke streaming from her nostrils.

"Ah, why am I telling you? How are you going to understand what it's like?"

But Lee did understand. She also understood that, deny it or not, Dorothy's rage was still burning brightly these several months later. It wasn't hard to imagine her smashing Kate's skull with the same intensity she'd used to demolish the butt. Lee hid a sudden shudder by taking another sip of her wine.

"Anyway," Dorothy continued, both hands around the squat highball glass, "yes, she offered to pay me." The whiskey was beginning to have its effect now. The lines of her face sagged, making her look more haggard than harsh, and her words had begun to slur. She downed what was left of the Scotch. "In that two faced, condescending way she had. God, she could be smug. I'll bet there are plenty of people who'd have been glad to bash her brains out if they had the chance." She tipped the empty glass to her mouth again, sucking at the ice. "Not that I'd expect you to admit it, being such bosom buddies. But a lot of people hated her guts, take it from me."

Lee wisely resisted two impulses: first, to come to Kate's defense; second, to ask where Dorothy had heard this oddly prevalent rumor that she and Kate had been so close. Instead she put down her wineglass and asked coolly, "Anyone in particular?"

Dorothy glared at her and set her glass down with a thump. "My advice to you," she said flatly, "is to stop playing Miss Marple, or whoever it is you're supposed to be, before you find your*self* dumped in a lake or something."

"But I'm not—"

"And in all the movies I see, the one asking the questions pays for the drinks." She stood abruptly and with a grimace she tossed her bill on the table. "Thanks a million, sport."

6

Lee sat at the table for some time after Dorothy left, staring dolefully into the bottom of her wineglass. So much for her first effort. She picked up the bar bills, winced, and turned them hurriedly facedown. She couldn't afford to do much more of this. Thirteen dollars and fifty cents for drinks—my God, fifteen dollars including a not-so-lavish tip—and she'd accomplished little more than antagonizing a veteran member of the tour, one who wouldn't hesitate to express her views on Lee Ofsted to anyone who cared to listen.

And that, she thought unhappily, was not a welcome prospect. As it was, she had a tough enough time making friends among her fellow golfers. It wasn't that she was a loner by nature. There were times, in fact, when she was sitting on an unsavory bed in some bargain motel on the outskirts of a town she didn't know, when the loneliness, the lack of anyone to really talk to, had almost been enough to make her give it all up and scuttle back to Portland, her tail between her legs.

The thing was, she simply didn't fit in; not with the country club pros' daughters who'd grown up breathing golf, and not with fresh-from-college players with their strings of regional amateur titles and their backers. Oh, it was easy enough to blend in physically. All you had to do was dig up the money to buy two or three reasonably fashionable outfits and you could pass. But when those feeling-out conversations started it was a different story. *What's your home club?* The North Portland Public Golf Course. *Where did you go to school?* For my A.A.? Army continuing ed. *What do your parents do?* My father lays cement, my mother's a housewife. *Where did you learn to play golf?* In the army, when I won a golf weekend at the Garmisch R and R facility with a two-dollar raffle ticket.

Talk about conversation-stoppers. The only people aside from Kate with whom she'd begun to develop any warmth were some of the other rabbits, a diminishing breed. And they, like her, missed the cuts so often, and had to break away from the tour to play in so many oddball, unofficial tournaments to earn enough to get by, that she often didn't see them for weeks at a time. And when she did, it would be just for a few days.

So, she philosophized gloomily, how much did it matter if Dorothy Kendall went around muttering that Lee Ofsted was nosing around in other people's affairs? There was going to be a lot of unpleasant gossip about her anyway soon enough. How long could it be before everybody from the players to the locker room attendants knew that the murder weapon had been found in her bag? What if the case was never solved? Would people be whispering and speculating about her from now on? Would she finally rate a decent-size gallery of her own, drawn by the thrill of getting close to an all-but-proven murderer? No, it didn't bear thinking about. Antagonizing a hundred Dorothy Kendalls was preferable by a long shot if it helped her get to the truth.

"That bad, huh?"

The throaty voice startled her. She looked up from the cocktail napkin she'd twisted into a spiral. "Oh, hi, Peg. Just getting in a little moping while I had the chance. What are you doing in a bar at two in the afternoon?"

"Looking for you. Not that I really expected to find you here." She flumped comfortably into Dorothy's recently vacated seat. "So tell me, what did Lieutenant Sheldon do to you? I see you're not in jail, anyway. That's something."

"Thanks for the vote of confidence. All Graham did was—"

" '*Graham*'?" Peg leaned forward with a grin. "You and the man of granite are on a first-name basis?"

Lee's forehead prickled with warmth. Now where had that come from? "Well, no, of course not, but he's not really so awful—"

"Who said anything about him being awful? Far from it! Come, tell me everything!"

"Come on, Peg, the man's investigating a murder, he's not on the make. What he did was buy me a hot dog, let me know that he thought I was innocent—"

"That was big of him."

"—and tell me to go play with my toys like a good girl and let the grownups take care of finding out who killed Kate."

Peg hesitated. "I don't know if I'd put it in those words," she said soberly, "but that sounds like a pretty good idea to me too."

"Oh, sure, and leave the whole investigation to Lieutenant Sheldon."

"Graham," said Peg.

"Peg, he doesn't know the first thing about golf."

"Maybe not, but does that really matter?"

"Of course it matters. If I hadn't explained in detail, he wouldn't have understood how I knew about the switched clubs. And he won't even think about any help from me—and I can help! That's what really fries me."

Peg studied her for a moment, her open face concerned. "Look, Lee, I think maybe you're letting this get to you more than you should. He's right; this isn't any of your business. Anyway, what can you do? On Monday you'll be off to your next tournament. Why not just let the police do their job?"

Lee shook her head. "No, Peg, I can't. And not just because I liked Kate. Don't forget that someone's out there trying to make me look like a murderer."

"Oh, come on, Lee, who's going to seriously believe—"

"And that's not all." She explained what she'd been moping about after her conversation with Dorothy Kendall.

That seemed to make an impression. Peg leaned back, her head tilted, considering. "Well, all right," she said slowly, "I guess I'd be concerned if I were you too, but—" She gestured at the nearly empty wineglass in front of Lee. "—boozing in the middle of the afternoon isn't going to help. It's not going to do your game any good either, Lee," she added solemnly.

Lee burst out laughing. "Don't jump to conclusions. This was in the line of duty." Briefly she told Peg about the unproductive interview. "I never even got around to finding out anything really important, like where she was yesterday evening. Not that she'd have told me. She'd probably have clipped me."

When the waitress came to their table, Lee shook her head. Peg ordered a double Wild Turkey on the rocks.

"Hey, wait a minute," Lee said. "I thought drinks in the middle of the afternoon ruin your golf game."

"They do, but who cares about *my* golf game? Anyway, I'm supposed to be having fun. You're not."

"That's a double standard."

"It sure is," Peg agreed cheerfully.

When the drink arrived she had a long, luxurious swallow. "Aahh. I've been thinking about that ever since I drove that stupid divot farther than the ball on the fourth." She dabbed at her lips with a cocktail napkin and sat back with a contented murmur.

"I sure blew it, didn't I?" Lee said glumly.

"You sure did. She didn't even pay her bill, did she?" Peg turned Dorothy's bar tab around to look at it. "My God, no wonder she's playing lousy golf."

Lee sighed. "I don't know where to go from here. I'd like to talk to Nick Pittman, but how do I get his attention? There are other people I need to talk to too, but everybody's up to their ears during the tournament. I just don't know how to go about it."

"I think I do," said Peg after a pause.

"You do?"

"Uh-huh." She took another long sip. "I know just the way we can get to the people we need to see."

Lee finished off the film of wine in the bottom of her glass and looked at Peg with a faint sense of misgiving. " 'We'?" she said in about the same tone Graham Sheldon had used with her a couple of hours before.

"Lee, if you don't think you can use some help, then you're as dense as your lieutenant."

"But—"

"Don't interrupt. You're based miles from everything, at that motel in Seaside. You don't have a car, for God's sake; how are you going to get around? And don't tell me you can afford to take taxis. You're—"

"But Peg, this could be . . ." Lee leaned forward and dropped her voice. It was going to sound theatrical enough as it was, without braying for everybody in the bar to hear. "This could be *dangerous*!"

"Naturally it could be dangerous. So?"

"So it's crazy for you to get involved."

"I'm already involved," Peg persisted stubbornly. "I was there when you found Kate, remember? That should entitle me to some of the excitement."

"Excitement . . . !" Lee laughed, half amused, half exasperated.

"There's something else I want to say, Lee. Now, don't take this wrong—" Peg shifted uneasily, had another gulp of whiskey, and plowed ahead. "—but if you think about it for a minute you'll realize you can't do it on your own. You can't get at the people you need to talk to. You just don't have the money or the clout to get into the circles that Kate moved in. Not yet, anyway," she added quickly. "It's just a question of time, of course."

Lee rotated her empty glass on the table in front of her. "I suppose you're right."

"Of course I am. You're still just a bunny; you can't get into the fancy dos."

"Rabbit, not bunny."

"Rabbit, bunny, what's the difference? In any case, I damn

well do have the clout, and I can use it to get you into the right places."

"I don't know," Lee said doubtfully. "If you're talking about society cocktail parties, I don't think I—"

"Now listen to me. A lot of the consulting for which I am paid so exorbitantly involves training managers to communicate. And among the wonderful things I teach them is how to create a climate that encourages open, honest expression without engendering hostility, recalcitrance, or other such bullshit."

"Yes, but—"

"And nothing in the world encourages such a climate more than a good party where everyone gets smashed. Trust me, I understand these things." She shifted in her seat, making bustly, authoritative sounds. "Now what I'm going to do is call Alma and get you invited to her buffet. That'll open up a lot of doors. Of course I'm already invited," she added modestly.

"Who's Alma?" It was Lee's turn to fidget uncomfortably. Things were starting to get away from her.

"Who's—" Peg stared at her. "Alma Harrington, who else?"

Lee sighed. "All right, who's Alma Harrington?"

Peg looked at her as if she'd asked who Babe Didriksen Zaharias was. "Alma Harrington," she said in measured tones, "is the Del Monte Forest's leading hostess, which makes her the Perle Mesta of the golf world. She's having one of her inimitable intimate gatherings tonight, which means something in the neighborhood of two hundred people lucky enough to be on her invitation list. Everybody who's anybody in the tournament. And I will bet you dollars to doughnuts that Kate O'Brian will be the number-one topic of conversation without us even having to mention her name." She raised her glass. "So, are you coming?"

Lee didn't need to think about it very long. "I'm coming," she said, and clinked her empty glass against Peg's. "It's funny to think," she said soberly, "that Kate's murderer is probably going to be there, sipping cocktails and making small talk."

"Are you saying you think whoever killed Kate is connected to the tournament?"

"Well, yes, I guess I do, don't you?"

"Not necessarily," Peg replied. "Don't forget about her playboy husband. He lives right here in Pacific Grove, doesn't he?"

Lee blinked. "I have no idea. Why would he want to kill her?"

"How would I know? We're just getting started. This is the exploring-possibilities phase." But a swallow of bourbon provided her with inspiration. "Wait a minute. Of course. California has community property law. With Kate dead he'd get half of her money instead of the piddling eighty thousand a year she's been doling out to him." She put the glass on the table with a clunk. "Right?"

Lee looked blankly at her. "Piddling eighty thousand a year she's been . . ."

"Doling out to him. They've been sort of informally separated for four years, you know, and she's been supporting him."

"No, I didn't know."

"And now," Peg said, gathering steam, "maybe she finally got up the nerve to divorce him, and he knew he'd be out in the rain. But if she just happened to die first, he'd wind up with more money than even *he* could spend—assuming she didn't have a will saying otherwise. Maybe he waited until she was alone in the fog, then snuck up—"

"Why didn't Kate divorce him years ago?"

"Supposedly," Peg said, "because she was such a staunch Catholic, but really because she still loved the bum."

Lee stared at her. "Peg, how do you know all that about Kate?"

"*People* magazine, *Parade*, *The National Enquirer*," Peg said with a shrug. "Various unassailable sources. You know, 'Secret Heartache Gnaws at Golf Superstar.' You mean you didn't know?"

Lee admitted sheepishly that she didn't. She had, in fact, known embarrassingly little about the murdered golfer, considering the time they'd spent together. She knew Kate was afraid of airplanes, which was why she drove to tournaments even though she could afford to fly easily enough, and she knew that Kate was married. But the two women had rarely talked about anything but golf on their drives, and sometimes not even that, since one of them—Lee, usually—often drove while the other slept.

"Well, then," Peg said, "it's a good thing that you've thrown your lot in with a walking encyclopedia of golf gossip. And there's plenty more where that came from."

"Wait a minute Peg," Lee said uncomfortably. "Should we really be digging into Kate's personal life? Shouldn't we leave that to Graham Sheldon? We only have a little time, and I think we better spend it following up on the golf aspects—which we understand but he knows beans about."

Peg sighed with resignation. "Boy, you want to take all the fun out of it. But, okay, you're right. We won't worry about Gilbert O'Brian." After another sip of bourbon she brightened. "Now, what about Dorothy Kendall? Did she actually threaten you?"

Lee hesitated. She wasn't really sure. "No, not exactly threatened me," she said. "She said I could wind up in a pond too if I wasn't careful."

"And you don't think that's a threat?"

"Well . . . it was the way she said it. Sort of generally. I didn't take it personally; not as a threat."

Peg studied her with pursed lips. "In my opinion," she said, "it is a very good thing indeed that you've enlisted my help. Now then. Would any other pros have had it in for Kate?"

Lee shrugged. "No one I can think of, really. Kate's personality ticked a lot of people off, but everybody was pretty much used to her."

When the waitress came to see about another round of drinks, Peg decided they needed something more substantial and ordered a platter of nachos to share.

"But, you know, there is one other person I've been wondering about," Lee said hesitantly when Peg turned back to her. "Nick Pittman."

"The tournament director? Was there bad blood between him and Kate?"

"Not so far as I know, but it sure seems to me that he went out of his way to implicate me in this mess. Maybe he was just trying to be helpful to the police, or maybe he just enjoys telling tales . . . or maybe he had an ulterior motive."

"For what? What'd he do?"

"Oh, he made sure Graham Sheldon knew I was on the tee with Kate just before she was killed. And he told him he overheard Milt Sawycr talking to me about some kind of endorsement deal that cut in on the arrangement they had with Kate."

"Huh?" The leather seat squeaked as Peg straightened up. "Is that true?"

"Yes, but you have to know Milt. That's just the way he talks. I wasn't paying any attention to him."

Peg laughed. "Believe it or not, I think I know what you mean; I once spent three consecutive minutes with him on a buffet line. But why would that implicate you? Do you mean it'd give you a reason for wanting Kate out of the way?"

Lee shrugged. "I guess so."

Looking absently over Peg's shoulder, she became aware that one of the beet-faced ladykillers in the bar was resolutely ogling her and had been at it for some time. She shifted to face away from him. "I mean, I can't really say that I think Nick killed anybody, but . . ." She let the sentence drift away, not sure what she did think.

"Yeah," Peg said with an equal lack of conviction.

The nachos arrived, and both women spent the next few minutes working on the fragrant mound of tortilla chips covered with a gummy accretion of what appeared to be everything left over from the previous day's Mexican plate special.

"Mm," Peg said, tugging a cheese-clotted chip from the pile. "Make sure you get some of the guacamole." She signaled the waitress again. "And a couple of bottles of Perrier," she called.

"No calories," she explained to Lee. "Look, what about Milt Sawyer? After all, he was talking about cutting Kate out. Could there be anything there?"

"I doubt it. I mean . . . *Milton Sawyer*?"

Peg smiled. "I admit it doesn't seem very credible, but let's keep him in mind. Let no one say we left any stone unturned."

Lee glanced at her watch. "Oh, gosh, I'm due at the police station in Carmel. I'm supposed to identify my three-wood." She piled refried beans on one last tortilla chip, swallowed it, and wiped her mouth.

"I'll drop you off," Peg said. "Then can you find your own way to my room at the lodge at about six? We can go from there."

"Sounds fine."

"Good. And that'll give me a couple of hours to do a little checking around on my own."

"On what?"

But Peg would only smile. "I'll tell you later," she said. "And I promise not to solve it all by myself."

7

GRAHAM MOTIONED TO the gray metal side chair across the desk. "Have a seat, Mr. Stratton. Thanks for coming in."

"No problem," Farley Stratton said with a shrug, settling down somewhat warily. "Never been in a police station before."

Graham smiled at him with a sort of satisfaction. Lee Ofsted had been playing hell with his stereotypes, but Stratton was reassuringly on the button; just what a Los Angeles-based sports star's agent ought to look like. Beefy and overweight, with a florid complexion only partly masked by a rich bronze coating straight out of a tanning lounge, he was built something like Dom De Luise and dressed something like Don Johnson. He wore a trendy off-white linen suit with what appeared to be a black tank top, soft, expensive moccasins without socks, and three or four thin, glistening gold chains sunk in the fleshy folds at his neck. Or maybe Don Johnson wasn't into chains, come to think of it. Give Farley Stratton credit for a unique fashion consciousness of his own.

"Any ideas for me on who might have killed Kate O'Brian, Mr. Stratton?"

"Nope. Everybody loved her. Greatest kid in the world."

"You never heard her say anything about having problems with someone?"

"Who doesn't have problems with someone? But no, nothing big."

"How long had you been her agent, Mr. Stratton?"

"Eight, eight and a half years. Manager, not agent."

"Sorry, I didn't realize there was a difference."

"Managers are more, like, proactive."

"Oh, proactive."

"Right."

"But you do the kinds of things agents do? Handle your client's business affairs?"

"You got it."

"That must be interesting."

He shrugged again. "It's a living. Okay if I smoke?"

Graham nodded and slid a square glass ashtray across the desk. Stratton pulled a pack of Marlboros from an inside pocket, flipped up the lid, and extracted a cigarette with his lips.

"Just out of curiosity," Graham said, "are you commissioned, or do you work on a salary?"

"I'm commissioned."

Graham waited, but nothing else was forthcoming. His interest quickened. It had been his experience that promoters, public relations people—and presumably managers—liked to talk, given a reason. Any time, any place, to anyone; even police officers.

"What percentage do you get?"

Stratton looked up from lighting the cigarette, his eyes squeezed almost shut against the smoke. "Just out of curiosity, right?"

"Pretty much." This was true. Graham believed in the fire-hose approach to interrogation. Spray all over the place, and sooner or later somebody was bound to get wet.

Stratton shrugged again, the third time in five minutes. That was a lot of shrugs. "I get twenty percent."

"Ah."

The heavy face flushed a shade more deeply. "That's standard."

"Is it? I thought it was ten to fifteen percent."

"That's what agents get. Managers get twenty."

"Because managers are more proactive?"

Stratton looked darkly at him and tapped his cigarette into the ashtray.

Graham knew well enough he was not winning a new friend, but he was already certain that the manager had something to hide, or at least something he was reluctant to talk about. Whether it had something to do with Kate O'Brian's murder was another question; homicide investigations routinely turned up astonishing numbers of things people wanted to keep hidden, and most of them weren't pertinent.

"Let's see . . ." Graham said, opening a folder and taking out the list of the WPGL's top-fifty money winners last year, which Rubio had photocopied from the latest *Golf Yearbook*. He let his finger run down a few spaces to O'Brian's name, as if he weren't already aware of the figure next to it—and of the fact that Stratton knew he knew. All part of the game.

"Three hundred and eighty-seven thousand dollars," he said. "That's a lot of money. So is twenty percent of three hundred and eighty-seven thousand dollars. Let's see now, that would be . . ." He raised his eyebrows, waiting for Stratton to finish it.

"Don't ask me," the manager said with a triumphant smile. All of his back teeth seemed to have gold crowns. "I don't have anything to do with tournaments. I don't get beans from a player's prize money."

"Oh?" That was a surprise.

"That's exactly right." Stratton nodded his head in brisk agreement with himself. "My percentage comes off the top of income *I* generate. Royalties and so on. Residuals. The only way I make money is to make money for my clients. Otherwise I don't get a dime." He tried a wry grin. "You're looking at a product of the ultimate merit system. No workee, no money."

"I see. Well, how much did you generate for Kate O'Brian last year?"

The grin faded. The product of the ultimate merit system shifted from one buttock to the other. "Jeez, it's hard to say exactly. I've got a lot of clients."

"You managed her business, you got twenty percent of it, and you don't know what she made?"

Stratton sucked in a terrific lungful of smoke, frowning, temporizing. "Well, you know—" The smoke poured out in a blue-gray explosion. "It's all like, fluid; it's hard to say at any particular point in time."

"You must have told the IRS something at several particular points in time."

He had thought that might strike a nerve, but it didn't. Stratton merely shrugged again. "For all intensive purposes," he said, "let's say about seven hundred thou. That's as close as I can come without my records."

Easy enough to check. Graham switched directions without warning. "What are you doing on the peninsula, Mr. Stratton?"

"What's that supposed to mean?"

It was Graham's turn to shrug. "You said you don't have anything to do with the tournaments. What brought you here?"

Stratton took another long pull on his cigarette, then slowly let the smoke out. "I had business; contract renewal talks with one of Kate's sponsors. We were gonna meet with them Thursday, yesterday."

"What company was that?"

"What's the difference? What's that got to do with anything?"

Graham waited patiently. He was beginning to wonder whether Stratton really had something on his mind or not. Maybe he was like this all the time.

"Sawyer," Stratton finally said grudgingly. "We flogged their golf equipment."

"On TV, you mean?"

"TV, magazines, you name it."

"And what would a contract like that be worth?"

"What do you mean, worth?"

"What were they paying her?"

"Why?"

Graham leaned forward and put both hands on the marbled beige Formica desktop. "Look, Mr. Stratton. You're not required to answer these questions. If you don't want—"

Stratton waved the cigarette in the air. "That's okay," he said hurriedly. "I guess this whole thing's got me shook up. What were they paying? I think—"

"You *think*? You flew up here to renegotiate a contract and you don't know what the arrangements were?"

"Well, these things are complicated. That's why I get twenty percent. See, it starts with a basic annual retainer—"

"All right, I'll settle for that. How much was the basic annual retainer?"

Stratton pulled a nonexistent shred of tobacco from his lip while he decided what to say. "Okay, I'm pretty sure it was a hundred and ten thou. I just didn't want to, you know, provide information off the top of my head that I wasn't a hundred percent sure of. I might be a little off."

"Mr. Stratton, when did you get here?"

"Wednesday morning" was the prompt response. "I flew PSA from L.A. to San Jose, then rented a Mercedes from Hertz and drove down." He was feeling on safer ground now, volunteering information.

"The day she was killed."

"Right. So?"

"Did you spend much time with her that day?"

"I didn't spend any time with her. We were supposed to meet Thursday. I already told you."

"What did you do Wednesday afternoon?"

"Played nine holes at Pebble Beach with a couple of other clients—I got other clients, you know—then took them out to dinner at Gallatin's." He stubbed his cigarette butt out in the ash tray. "I got about three thousand witnesses."

Graham laughed. "I'm glad to hear it. Look, Mr. Stratton, I have a hunch I'll want to talk with you again. Are you going to be here for a while?"

"Through Sunday. I've got some meetings set up."

"That's fine. Well, thanks for coming in. I enjoyed talking to you."

"Yeah," said Stratton glumly, getting slowly to his feet. "Likewise."

A few seconds later Rubio tapped at the glass pane in the door to Graham's transparent cubicle, then walked in without waiting. Graham was pleased. The sergeant was getting more assertive.

Rubio jerked his head in the direction of the departing Stratton. "How'd it go? Come up with anything?"

"Could be."

"Well, you must have scared him. He looked pretty nervous going out," said Rubio, who was unquestionably an expert in nervous looks.

"I think he was ripping off Kate O'Brian one way or another. Maybe some of his other clients too."

Rubio's eyebrows knitted. "Then why didn't you—"

"Easy, Gerald. That doesn't mean he killed her. That means we want to do a little more checking on him. Let's talk about it first thing tomorrow morning."

Graham looked at his watch. "Four-fifteen," he said, rising and slipping the few notes he'd made into the center drawer of his desk. "I have to talk to someone at four-thirty, so—"

"Gilbert O'Brian's here to see you. That's what I came in to tell you."

"Kate's husband? I thought he was coming in tomorrow." He flipped a page in his calendar pad with the eraser of a pencil. "At ten-thirty."

"I know, but he just dropped in now. He said it was more convenient."

"Just like that?"

"Well, he said he had to come to Carmel anyway to get a

few outfits fitted at Ralph Lauren's, so he thought that while he was downtown he might as well—"

"It didn't occur to him," Graham snapped, "to keep his appointment here tomorrow and just 'drop in' on Ralph Lauren while he was in town then?"

Graham was annoyed with himself for being irritated. He knew precisely what was bothering him. Partly it was a cop's automatic response to anyone who treated his case with less than proper respect. Partly it was his instinctive if absurd reaction to someone who had his "outfits" fitted, and got them at Ralph Lauren's to boot. And partly it was a defensible but pointless antagonism toward a man who saw his wife's murder as something to drop in and chat about when it was convenient.

But mostly it was because his four-thirty appointment had been with Lee Ofsted.

POLICE DEPARTMENT, CARMEL-BY-THE-SEA, the raised metal letters on the neat, white retaining wall said. That was nice. Better than plain old Carmel.

The wall separated a flower bed from a sweeping brick and concrete-slabbed terrace laid out in front of the low building at the corner of Fourth and Junipero. Whoever had designed it had managed to create a simple, graceful building that looked functional and serious, yet somehow managed to blend in with the doll-house architecture and mock-Tudor half-timbering that were Carmel's trademarks.

It was the first time Lee had been in a police station, and after she gave her name to the grandmotherly woman in a mauve pantsuit who was at the counter (what had happened to the grizzled sergeants that were supposed to man the desks?), she glanced around with open curiosity. But she'd barely begun to look at the stately, framed photographs of Carmel's past police chiefs when she sensed someone come up behind her.

She turned with a smile, but it wasn't Graham. It was a sergeant, but not a grizzled one. Not even a uniformed one. It was Sergeant Rubio, frowning worriedly at her.

"What—what's wrong?" she asked.

"Wrong?" he said, and the question seemed to startle him. "Nothing's wrong." His eyebrows knit closer still. "Is there?"

Sergeant Rubio's apprehensiveness, she began to see, was more a matter of manner than substance. "No, everything's fine, as far as I know. I'm supposed to see Lieutenant Sheldon."

He shook his head darkly. "The lieutenant's tied up. You're here to identify the club, right? I can show it to you."

Lee nodded, annoyed with herself for being so disappointed, and followed Sergeant Rubio down a short corridor, past an ordinary wooden door with a neat plastic plate that said "Holding Cell." (Didn't they have bars, or grilles, or slots to pass in trays of greasy chicken and mashed potatoes? She was definitely going to have to up-date her information about the criminal justice system.) Next to this door was an unmarked one, which Sergeant Rubio opened to reveal a room not much larger than a walk-in closet, lined by waist-high cupboards topped with a stainless steel counter. The sight of Kate's big red-and-white Wilson golf bag, water-stained and forlorn, lying on the counter not far from her own, shocked her unexpectedly. Where was Kate's body right now? she wondered. Also lying on a stainless steel counter somewhere? Locked away in a refrigerated drawer in some basement? She shivered.

"You recognize either of these bags?" Sergeant Rubio asked.

"Yes, of course. That one's mine. This is Kate's." *Was* Kate's, she was going to have to learn to say.

"Can you identify any of the clubs in the decedent's bag as your own?"

"You mean you don't know which one it's supposed to be?"

"Of course I know," he said, mildly offended. "But I can't tell *you* which one it is before you tell *me*. What kind of an identification would that be?"

Lee accepted the rebuke quietly. It wasn't going to be much of an identification anyway, when it came down to it. Unless there was more than one three-wood in the bag, it was pretty obvious which club was supposed to be hers.

She looked at the heads of the clubs protruding from the bag, oddly reluctant to touch them. Only the irons had been unaffected by the water. The woods were another story. Normally their gleaming, pressure-impregnated finish made them impervious to moisture and eliminated the old problems of swelling, shrinking, and warping. But they hadn't yet designed finishes to withstand overnight soakings in lakes.

She pulled the spongy, cracked three-wood from the bag. Irreparable, and it was going to cost plenty to replace it, she thought guiltily (Why wasn't she thinking about poor Kate, not her budget?), and even with a new club from the same line, the balance would never exactly match that of the others. Turning it upside-down, she examined the area to the left of the sole plate.

"It's mine. Here's the nick I got in New Jersey a couple of months ago."

"I'm afraid we'll have to keep it for evidence," Sergeant Rubio said, worried again.

"In this condition it's not much of a loss." Lee handed it back to him and put her hand on her bag. "I hope you don't have to keep my others."

This was a new and serious problem for Sergeant Rubio. He pursed his lips and considered. "I think you'll have to ask the lieutenant about that."

"The lieutenant says she's welcome to them. The lab's finished with them."

She turned at the sound of Graham Sheldon's voice to see him standing in the corridor just outside the door, next to an extraordinarily handsome man in white jeans, huaraches, and a formidably expensive-looking, bulky-knit sweater with loose raglan sleeves down to his tan, well-muscled forearms. For a moment she thought she'd seen him before, and in a way, she realized, she had. He looked like a mannequin in an upscale men's boutique.

Literally. From the thick, layered auburn hair that managed to look wind-touseled and exquisitely groomed at the same time to the slim, gracefully canted hips that radiated sexuality and self-assurance. Even the twin creases, loaded with mature charm and masculinity, that ran from the corners of crinkly blue eyes to either side of the craggy jawline were there. He was, she thought, possibly the best-looking man she had ever seen. If you were partial to mannequins.

He smiled at her and the sunny crinkles around his eyes deepened. "Well, hi there. You're Lee Ofsted, aren't you?" His voice was about what you'd expect a mannequin's voice to be like if it had one: deep and rich, but somehow a little hollow.

"Thanks very much for coming in, Mr. O'Brian," Graham said with a somewhat stiff smile, guiding him away from the room with a firm hand at the elbow.

O'Brian? Was this Kate's husband? No wonder she'd been smitten.

"Wait a minute," he said. "That's Kate's bag. . . ."

The pressure of Graham's hand increased and O'Brian gave way, listing to the right.

"I'll be in touch," Graham said. "Sergeant, would you see Mr. O'Brian out?"

"I can find my own way out," O'Brian said evenly.

"That's all right," the tone was pleasant but inflexible. "Gerald?"

Reluctantly O'Brian left with Sergeant Rubio.

"Was *that* Gilbert O'Brian?" Lee asked when they were out of earshot. "Wow. He's spectacular-looking."

"I suppose so" was the somewhat cross reply. "If you like the type."

"Is he a suspect? I mean, he had a reason to kill Kate didn't he?"

Graham's eyebrow lifted.

"Just curious, that's all," she said quickly. "You hear these rumors."

"I see. Well, to satisfy your curiosity, yes, he had a reason, and yes, he's a suspect, but he gave me the name of a woman who was supposed to verify his presence in her apartment Wednesday evening, and yes, I've already called her and she does verify it, but no, I'm not inclined to take it at face value, and I have more checking to do, which I have already set in motion, using some of the many advanced methods of criminal detection that are at my disposal." He stopped to take a breath. "Anything else you're curious about?"

Lee shook her head mutely. At least she'd been right about leaving Kate's personal life to the police. "Well, one thing," she said on second thought. "Did the lab find anything funny about my clubs?"

"Nothing at all. There's no reason to think the killer did anything more than switch the two clubs and then toss Kate's bag into the water." He shook his head. "Damn lucky to get away with it without being seen."

"Yes, I keep thinking about that. Even with the fog, you'd think someone in the pro shop would have seen something out the window."

"Probably would have if not for the pigeon."

"Pigeon?" she said, puzzled. "Is that police slang for something?"

He laughed. "Yes, for a fat gray bird that eats peanuts and likes to sit on statues. It got into the pro shop the day before and took up residence on a shelf on top of the sport shirt rack. They thought it might be sick, so they called the SPCA in Salinas to come pick it up, which they did. But then it got loose in Salinas and flew back to the sport shirts—unfortunately for us, just a little before five o'clock. At the time Kate was murdered the assistant pro was apparently on the phone trying to get in touch with the SPCA again, the clerk was trying to coax the bird down with some Cracker Jacks, and the four customers were all holding out their fingers and going 'coo, coo.' So nobody was looking out the window."

She stared at him. "That's just crazy enough to be true. Talk about rotten coincidences."

He grinned back at her. "Yes, or of course the pigeon may have been an accomplice. I'll give it the third degree as soon as it's well." He looked at his watch. "I have to go talk to

Nick Pittman at Carmel Point. Can I give you a lift that way?"

"Thanks, that'd be nice."

He hefted her bag from the counter to his shoulder.

"Carry your clubs for you? Or don't you like that kind of thing?"

"Carry away," she said. "I'm liberated only up to a point."

They were in the car turning out into Junipero Avenue before Lee realized that something had been bothering her about the club-swing.

"Lieutenant," she said slowly, "I don't understand why the killer went to the trouble of switching the three-woods. How could he know—"

"Or she."

"Or she," Lee agreed. "How could they assume you'd ever find out about it? I mean, I could just as easily not have seen the blood and simply tossed it into my locker. Or if I did realize it, what was to stop me from keeping it to myself instead of being dumb enough to call the police and incriminate myself? Either way, no one would have found out about it, and I'd never come under suspicion. So what was the point?"

He nodded briefly at her. "That was bothering me too. Until I got back to my office after lunch."

"What happened when you got back to your office?"

"There was a letter waiting for me. Mailed in Carmel, and anonymous, of course. It said you had something to hide and—à la *The Purloined Letter*—it was right out in the open in your golf bag, and we'd better go get hold of it." He smiled. "Of course, the writer had no way of knowing you'd already been dumb enough to call us, which totally spoiled the effect."

Lee frowned. That settled it beyond a shadow of a doubt. Someone was trying very actively to pin this thing on her. And not any too subtly either.

"Can you trace it?" she asked. "Fingerprints, or the stationery, or the handwriting . . ."

He shook his head. "No prints, good old Walgreen stationery, and block letters. Forget it."

"An anonymous letter," Lee mused. "This may be everyday life to you, but it gets more unreal by the minute to me." She turned in her seat to look at him. "What would have happened if you'd gotten the letter first? Would you have had to arrest me?"

"Not a chance," he said simply.

She sighed quietly. Thank goodness it was Graham who was handling this case and not some stiff, by-the-book cop who had no pleasant intuitions about her, and wouldn't have trusted them if he did.

Her thoughts must have shown. "But don't think you're getting any special treatment," he said. "You better believe I'd have checked it out, but I'd have been just as interested—more interested—in who wrote the letter. Who, by the way, I'm starting to think may be lucky but not very bright. He should be lying low, not muddying the water. Now where can I drop you off?"

"The clubhouse will be fine. I have a set of good clothes in my locker for emergencies, and I can get the courtesy van to the lodge from there. Peg Lathan's taking me to a party."

"Just what you need," he said warmly, turning into the North San Antonio Avenue entrance to the course and driving up the serene, cypress-lined main drive. "It'll do you good to forget about this for a while. It won't hurt my peace of mind either."

"Your peace of mind?" she said, deciding to play dense.

"Yes. Something tells me you don't always listen to advice, even from those wiser and older than you."

"How old are you?" she asked impulsively.

"Thirty-one."

A nice age, it seemed to her. "You're older," she agreed.

"And wiser."

Lee was silent.

"About certain things, anyway," he persisted with a cursory gesture at modesty. "And my advice remains the same. Stay away from deserted tees and don't go poking around doing any muddying of your own. Sipping champagne and eating canapés in the middle of a crowd is a very sensible thing to do with your time."

"Good," she said. "I'm glad that you approve. That's just what I intend to do."

8

"I JUST FEEL like a rat," Lee said, frowning down at her cup. "I really hated lying to him." She stirred a second packet of sugar into the tea, something she rarely did, but it had been another long day. Was it really only this morning she'd found the bloodstained club?

"You did not lie," Peg said in her sensible way. "You told him you were going to a party. You *are* going to a party, aren't you? You just didn't bother him with a lot of inessential details, that's all."

"I doubt if he'd see it quite that way."

With a wave of her hand Peg dismissed the lieutenant's reservations. "You'll be happy to know, by the way, that I kept my promise." She uncrossed her sturdy ankles, crossed them the other way, and resettled her square, stockinged feet on the butler's table in front of the small gray sofa.

"What promise?"

"Not to solve the case on my own. Not," she muttered, "that I didn't give it a good try."

Lee looked warily at her. "All right, Peg, what have you been up to?"

"Well," Peg said, cradling her cup on her lap with both hands, "I called this contact I have who knows everything that's going on in the business end of sports and asked a few pertinent questions about Kate's financial portfolio."

"I thought," Lee said, "that we'd agreed to stay out of her personal life."

"Who's talking about her personal life? I'm talking about golf. Kate's money was all golf-related: prize money, endorsements, royalties, residuals, investments. Money, as you may have noticed, is a major motive for those in professional sports."

"So I've heard," Lee said. "I wouldn't know from personal experience."

"Your time will come," Peg said comfortably. "Now, money also happens to be a major incentive for murder, *n'est ce pas*? So I asked my reliable but anonymous source if anything—oh, interesting—was happening. You know, squabbles over fees, contract disputes, nasty litigation, and such." She finished her tea and looked into the ceramic teapot. "You want me to send down for some more?"

Lee shook her head. She was sitting in a blue velour French Provincial armchair opposite Peg. Behind the older woman the French doors looked out over the last of a September twilight on the broad, forest-lined sweep of Carmel Bay, a hundred shades of deep, luminous blue, like a picture made of butterfly wings. The Motel 6 in Seaside looked out on a pizza parlor.

"Peg," Lee said dreamily, "how much does this room cost?"

"Around three hundred a day. Why?"

Lee sighed. With the help of a hefty discount from the sympathetic manager she was paying $11.40 a night. "No reason. Just wondering."

Peg studied her for a few seconds. "Ofsted, I'm starting to think you have a negative and somewhat counterproductive attitude about money."

"Gee, I wonder why that is. Well, tell me. What did you find out from your reliable source?"

Peg made a face. "Nothing. Apparently Kate got along better with her business associates than with golfers and reporters. Very disappointing. By the way, did you know she was going to retire after this season?''

''No,'' Lee said, surprised. ''I knew she was getting tired of the grind. She played in only nine or ten tournaments all season. But she never said a word about quitting.''

''Well, it's true. About a year ago she started taking over her own money management bit by bit, to give herself something to do after she quit. And it looks like she had a flair for it, because she was doing great.''

Lee bit thoughtfully at her lower lip. ''Wait a minute, Peg. Maybe you did find something.''

''I did?''

''Maybe someone didn't want Kate to retire, someone whose income depended on her playing.''

''Like who? I mean whom.''

''I don't know. Like . . . Well, like Ben, her caddie.''

Peg laughed. ''Come on, I thought *I* was reaching. Ben's a fixture on the tour, you know that. 'Gentle Ben,' they call him. He's supposed to be the nicest man in golf. Can you really see him as a vicious killer?''

''No, but can you see Nick as one? I mean, really. Or Milt? Dorothy Kendall? Nobody you know ever *seems* like a killer.'' She reconsidered. ''Well, on second thought, maybe Dorothy.''

''I agree, but getting back to Ben: Don't professional caddies get the same standard salary, whoever they're carrying for? Whomever? Whoever?'' She jerked her head irritably. ''The hell with it. Anyway, why would Ben be mad enough to kill her? Why wouldn't he just find someone else to pack a bag for? All those years with Kate O'Brian would probably make him a pretty desirable catch for some young pro who doesn't know the ropes.''

''No, it doesn't work that way. The weekly salary's roughly the same, yes—two or three hundred—but you're forgetting about his five percent of her winnings over and above that.'' Lee's voice grew a little more excited. She had thrown out Ben's name only half seriously, but now she didn't know. ''Last year Kate was third on the money list with almost four hundred thousand dollars. Five percent of that is—is . . . what? You're the financial expert."

"Twenty thousand smackers," Peg said without hesitation. She tilted her head sideways. "You're right. That's probably big money for a caddie."

"You bet it is," Lee said. It wouldn't be small change to some golfers she could think of either, but she kept that point to herself, not wanting Peg to think she was being counterproductive again. "And now that I think about it, I haven't seen Ben around these last couple of days."

"Why would he be around without Kate?"

"Well, you'd think he'd be looking for someone else to carry for now that she's not there anymore. Even one of the amateurs, maybe, if it was too late to line up a pro. But the last time I saw him was—my God." She put the cup and saucer down carefully on the low table. "The last time I saw him was near the clubhouse a little before Kate was killed. I remember that it struck me as odd because he wasn't there picking up for Kate when she was practicing."

"I'll say it's odd," Peg said enthusiastically. "I think we've got something to look into here."

Lee shook her head vigorously. "I think," she said, "we've got some information to pass on to Lieutenant Sheldon. He already knows I saw Ben there, but I think I better tell him what we've just been talking about."

"Fine, but that doesn't mean we can't do a little sensitive probing of our own, does it?"

"Peg, I'm not trying to be some kind of heroine," Lee said firmly. "I just want to see the murderer caught."

"Who's talking about heroines? I'm not suggesting meeting Ben at the twelfth tee at midnight, you know. I'm just talking about seeing what we can find out in our own subtle and delicate way."

"I suppose you're right," Lee said doubtfully.

"Of course I am." She stroked her lower lip with a forefinger. "You know, there's someone else who stood to lose a lot if Kate took over her own affairs."

Lee looked inquiringly at her.

"Her manager," Peg said.

"Farley Stratton? I don't know; I admit the guy's a little unappetizing, but—"

"He gets twenty percent of her earnings, right? Aside from prize money."

"I suppose so. That's pretty standard."

"Well, then, we're talking about a lot of money, and let's not forget that Farley's been on the skids for a few years, ever since he started hitting the bottle. And Kate was the only really big-time client he had left after that fighter, Jawbreaker Something, left him. Or was it Headcrusher?"

"I have no idea. That anonymous source of yours seems to have a lot of information."

Peg shook her head. "Straight out of *The National Investigator*: 'Superjock Dumps Superagent; "No Booze Hound for Me," Boxer Says.' " She frowned. "Wait a minute, though. What are we talking about? What good would it do Farley to kill her? Or Ben, for that matter. They'd still be out in the cold."

"Yes, but remember, everything about the murder points to its being a spur-of-the-moment thing. Maybe they argued, maybe they fought. Who knows, maybe Farley was drunk."

"Ah," Peg said with satisfaction. "True." She wiggled her toes, studying them with interest, then looked at her watch. "Party time." She fished under the sofa for her shoes and squeezed into them with a grimace.

"Well, shall we go and mingle with the *haut monde* and see what we can see?"

This was a welcome new side to the golf life. Feeling chic and sensual, Lee sipped champagne from a hollow-stemmed goblet—glass, not plastic—and glanced around the opulent room. Even for Del Monte Forest, the Harrington's Italianate Rococo mansion was something. She knew it was Italianate Rococo because when she and Peg had been caught in a bottleneck at the massive entrance she'd heard someone say, "Oh, yes, I suppose it's all very well if what you want is an Italianate Rococo mansion." Somehow Lee had managed to keep a straight face.

With most of the other guests, she was in what could have

been a ballroom but must have been the living room: softly gleaming hardwood floors, Persian carpets, gilt and antiques, marble busts of Roman emperors (Greek statesmen?) in smooth oval niches above the doors. From the vantage point she'd chosen for herself near the monumental marble fireplace she could see five of the world's top ten women golfers. There were television and movie personalities holding court, a senator, and even most of a famous punk rock group over in a corner by themselves, clinking their chains and working at looking malevolent.

But the bits of conversation audible over the general hubbub were no different from what could be heard at the far less trendy parties she sometimes got to attend after tournaments, or, for that matter, in any golf club locker room on any nice afternoon. The participants were dissecting their day's play.

". . . My God, Ellen, here I am stacking up birdies on fourteen through sixteen, figuring I've got it made—I mean, wouldn't you?—and then on the seventeenth I hit the ball out of bounds three times in three shots, and then, if you can believe it, this idiot jogger . . ."

". . . Cora, I'm telling you, it's a historical first. I'll be in the *Guinness Book of Records*. *Anybody* can hit out of a sand trap onto the green, but who did you ever hear of who putted from the green into a sand trap? I still don't know whether to laugh or to . . ."

Lee smiled. Disasters recounted—the staff of life at the nineteenth hole. Whatever their faults, golfers were certainly not braggarts. Masochists, maybe, but not braggarts. They loved to talk about their foul-ups. Even the occasional tale of triumph was usually attributed more to divine intervention or blind luck than skill.

". . . caught the ball with heel of my sand wedge and it was shooting straight for the bunker on the *other* side of the green, when it hits the flag stick four feet off the ground and going about a hundred miles an hour. Two crazy bounces and plop, right in the hole. Sal practically swallowed her teeth. . . ."

Lee didn't blame the amateur players for milking their

day's golf for all it was worth. They'd forked over $2,500 apiece for the chance to tee up with a pro in actual competition and perhaps be seen playing on television. They would have been working hard on their games—taking crash lessons or reading those impossible books. ("At this point, the shoulders should rotate independently of the hips, on a plane matching the angle of the arms to the ball at the time of address. This will be easily accomplished if you imagine that you are standing in a barrel, with an elastic band holding your forearms together, and an iron rod connecting the tip of your chin . . .")

Peg sauntered over, looking very much at her ease. "I'm starving. How about some munchies while we wait for the war stories to die down?"

"What makes you think they ever will?" Lee grumbled.

"Don't despair," Peg said. "Trust to serendipity."

When they had threaded their way to one of the four buffet tables, Lee found herself next to a ruddy, frowning man in a dove-gray dinner jacket: Nick Pittman, focusing his considerable reserves of anxiety and indecision in an intense study of the cheese tray. He was apparently alone.

Peg, with her plate already loaded, flashed her a lightning-quick what-did-I-tell-you grin and made a diplomatic retreat.

"Hi, Nick," Lee said.

He looked somewhat vaguely at her. In his hand he held a plate with a few rounds of French bread. "Oh, hello, uh, Lee," he said after a moment's hesitation, and returned to his profound examination of the cheeses.

That was informative right there. You wouldn't think that someone who went to a lot of trouble to frame you for murder would have trouble placing you. On the other hand, if he were guilty, what cleverer way would there be for him to act?

She leaned over beside him and looked at the array of exotic cheeses. "Where'd they put the Velveeta?" she asked.

He laughed. So far, so good.

"I'm at a complete loss," she said. "Could you recommend one of them?"

If he was taking all that time to study them, she reasoned, he must know something about them. Speaking for herself, they looked awful—blue-veined, green-veined, oozy, spotted with gruesome black mold. And the smell reminded her of the time she'd opened a locker to find it stuffed with clothes used during a rainy tournament three months before.

"Well, now," he said slowly, and she knew she'd started off right. "You have certainly come to the right person." Already he seemed less anxious than she'd ever seen him. With astonishing decisiveness, he spooned up a gob of runny yellow muck from a sagging wedge on the second level of the lazy Susan. Lee flinched. Risking her life was one thing, but this she hadn't bargained for.

But he smeared it on some bread on his own plate, popped it into his mouth, and smiled. He was showing off. "Not for beginners," he said.

Thank God.

"No, you'll want to work up to the Brie de Meaux," he said, chewing. "I think you could start with . . ." He spun the lazy Susan with considerable flair—he was a very different Nick Pittman tonight—and stopped it with a finger. ". . . this Reblochon." He pointed to an inoffensive-looking round cheese with an orange rind. "Vaguely reminiscent of a Camembert—you know Camembert?—but much milder."

She was in luck. He was the sort of man who liked to instruct. Docilely she cut through the crust, pared off a sliver, spread it on a soft slice of bread at his instruction, and took a gingerly bite. Not too bad. At least it didn't smell as if it had sat in a locker for three months.

Nick beamed his approval. "Now I think a Tomme de Savoie, but you have to approach this properly."

He waved over a waiter who was floating majestically through the crowd with a tray of wine. In doing so, Nick spilled the remnants of his own wine on her—fortunately, on the back of her hand, not her dress—and she realized suddenly why he seemed so relaxed and different. Nicholas Shapeworthy Pittman III was smashed. She looked at him curiously. She hadn't taken him for a drinker.

Well, she supposed he deserved his night to howl, considering the strain of putting on his first big-time tournament. And it wasn't going to hurt her sleuthing any to have him a little off his guard and extra-friendly.

Things were looking up.

"Red wine with cheese," he proclaimed, handing her a glass and taking one for himself.

"Yes, sir," Lee said, and Nick laughed and downed a hearty slug.

They worked their way through three or four more kinds of cheese, with Lee managing to avoid the Brie by surreptitiously nudging the lazy Susan around every time he got close. Between bites and sips she let him lead the talk, which went from cheese to wine to his import business.

"Do you know," he said, his words slurring more and more, "that in a very real . . . way, Europa Distributors is responsible for your being . . . being here right now?"

"No," Lee said. "Really?"

He nodded vigorously. "Yup. If I didn't make a quarter of a mill—" He smiled slyly at her and waggled his finger. "—a lot of money from it, I couldn't afford a member . . . membership at Carmel Point, now could I? And if I, if I couldn't afford a mum . . . mem . . . then I wouldn't be chairman of the Carmel Point board of d'rectors, would I? Hm? And if I wasn't chairman of the, of the . . . well, then I wouldn't be the tournament chairman, I mean champion, I mean director, because, because . . . Well, you see what I mean. We wouldn't be having this wonderful tourma . . . tournament."

No, she didn't see, but she smiled encouragingly.

Surprisingly, his face clouded. "I guess it's not really so wonderful, is it? Not with . . . not with Kate O'Brian's . . . not with her . . . uh . . ."

"Murder," Lee supplied when she couldn't stand it any longer. He had finally come around to what she wanted to talk about but now it was going to get trickier. She set her barely touched glass on the tablecloth.

"Yes, that was awful," she said. "You know, I've figured out just where I was when she died. I was in the clubhouse, right on the course."

And where were you? She didn't dare ask him, but she focused all her mental energy on willing him to answer. When he didn't, she prompted him a little more. "Yes, I was just a few hundred yards from where it happened."

"Um," he said, looking thoughtful.

She was going to have to do a lot better than that. If he *had* killed Kate, he was hardly going to admit he was up there on the practice tee with her, but if he came up with a lie, he might well make some telltale slip that would come out when she checked on his story. He was certainly in no condition to be particularly wily.

"I suppose you were at some important committee meeting or something," she said brightly.

"Um," he said again. "Yes, 's right. Some im . . . imp'nt c'mittee meeting." He frowned hard, then cocked his head wonderingly. "Wasn't I?"

Either he was fading fast or he was a hell of an actor. Lee was going to have to be more direct, like it or not. She stopped his hand as he raised the wineglass—his second since they'd begun talking—to his mouth.

"Nick," she said firmly, "why did you tell the police that Milt Sawyer and I were talking contracts that night at the restaurant?"

He narrowed his eyes and looked at her for a long time, swaying slowly from side to side. " 'Cause," he said gravely, " 's what you were doing."

And that was all she could get from him before two members of the pin placement committee dragged him off to discuss some pressing problem. Silently she wished them better luck than she'd had getting anything coherent out of him. She had hoped to get his answers to two questions: Where had he been when Kate was killed? And why had he made a point of telling Graham Sheldon about her conversation with Milt?

Well, she'd had twenty minutes alone with him, and she'd gotten answers to both questions. And she still didn't know anything she hadn't known before, which wasn't much.

Not a very auspicious start, but she wasn't about to give up after a single failure. She left her wineglass on the table, then had a glass of ginger ale, a deviled egg, and a couple of rice crackers with shrimp spread to fortify herself (and wash away the lingering taste of the cheese), and walked resolutely into the crowd, striking up conversations with almost everyone she knew and quite a few she didn't. To little avail.

People were surprisingly willing to talk about Kate, but what they wanted to do was ask questions, not answer them. Everybody seemed to be under that odd illusion that she and Kate were best friends. She tried to talk to Dorothy Kendall again, but all it earned was a poisonous stare and a sarcastic comment, which was about all she'd really expected.

It had been a snap to waylay Milt Sawyer—getting away was another story—but when she subtly brought the subject around to Sawyer Sporting Equipment's relationship with Kate, his pink, shiny baby's face had gone wooden.

"I am not," he informed her, "at liberty to discuss the contractual arrangements made by our company at this time."

Uh-huh, Lee thought, meaning Papa Sawyer had told his loquacious offspring to stop throwing offers and proposals around in his name without prior consultation. It was rumored in the trade that such paternal talking-tos were periodically necessary.

"Sorry," she said. "I didn't mean to pry." She noted with mixed feelings that the offer he had made to her the other evening was not repeated.

"Did you manage to find a replacement for Kate on *Golf World*?" she asked, trying to open him up. "Could you get hold of Arnie or Seve?"

"That didn't work out," he said tersely. "We ran a file tape on snow golf in Lapland."

And that ended that. It was when she was turning away from Milt that she bumped heavily, chest to chest, into a burly, blowzy man with a double whiskey in his hand.

"I'm sorry," she said.

"I'm not." The man grinned. "Any time. Best thing that's happened to me all night." He took a thorough if bleary look at her and widened the grin. Gold gleamed at the back of his mouth. "Lee, hey, how're you doing, babe? I heard you were here. You look great!"

"Farley?" she managed to squeak. "Farley Stratton?" Talk about serendipity.

"Sure. Hey, are you here with anyone? I mean, where are you going after this? You need a lift?"

"No, I'm fine, thanks. I'm so sorry about Kate. I know you two were close. She always spoke very highly about you."

Kate, as a matter of fact, had rarely had a good word for him, but Lee supposed that a small lie for the greater good was in order.

It did not, however, elicit any openness from Farley, who shrugged. "Yeah, it's tough. I hear you're the one who found her."

"Yes."

"Rough, babe."

"Yes, it was." She appraised him thoughtfully. He was not as far gone as Nick, or maybe he just held his liquor better, but this was most certainly not his first double of the night.

"Farley, who do you think could have killed her? Was there anything on the business end that might have led to it? I don't know, a dispute over a contract, or a . . . a . . ." Her imagination failed her; she had exhausted her knowledge of the business end.

"Nah, you're fishing up the wrong tree," said Farley, who had a way with metaphors. "It's probably some other golfer she screwed one time or another. Let's not kid ourselves; Kate was a hell of an athlete, but she wasn't exactly Little Miss Charming."

"I know."

His mood altered subtly. A blind seemed to come down over his eyes. "Dottie Kendall told me you were going around grilling people."

"I'm not. I mean . . . Farley, I'm just trying to answer some questions in my own mind."

It hadn't been a winning explanation when she'd used it with Dorothy, and it didn't do any better this time.

"Yeah, well, if I was you," Farley said, "I'd leave it to the police. You stick your nose into things and somebody's liable to get nervous and go after you too."

No, it was definitely not a line she would use again.

Farley put his hand on Lee's upper arm and shifted her a little to the side, effectively cornering her against the wall. The hand lingered overlong on her bare flesh, the thumb gently stroking the inside of her elbow.

Lee was more uneasy than frightened. She had met Kate's manager twice before, and both times he had tried to date her. Each time she had turned him down. In addition to being generally unappetizing, Farley was married; on an otherwise bronzed hand there was a pallid band of skin around his finger where he wore his wedding ring when he wasn't traveling. Lee was not without standards, even when it came to free meals, and this kind of oily creepiness was below them.

"Uh, look," he said, and the thumb moved in broader circles, "if you really want to know, I guess we could go over Kate's business stuff together. Uh, why don't you come over to my place for a drink, and I'll uh, clue you in?"

"Uh," she said, managing to get her arm out of his grasp, "your place?"

"I've got a suite at the lodge. Fantastic, five hundred a day. We could talk."

This was progress, but she wasn't about to go anywhere alone with him. "Thanks, Farley, but I'm here with a friend. Maybe we could—"

"Well, after it's over, then." He grinned slackly. "I don't like to go to bed until pretty late."

Did he really find her so attractive? She didn't think so. Farley was one of those men who did this automatically, like the café-loungers she remembered from an Army bus tour to Rome; men who considered it an obligation, no matter how exhausted or preoccupied they might be, to bestow on every female, whatever her age or appearance, a feverish and slack-jawed gaze of unfathomable longing. She doubted, in fact, that Farley would be much of a threat if she took him up. He'd probably be too amazed.

But she wasn't going to chance it. "No, I can't, Farley. Could we maybe have a drink together—"

He gave her an unconvincingly wolfish leer.

"—at the Cormorant Room after tomorrow's round?"

"You don't trust me, huh?" he said, still smiling, but she was sure he was relieved. She would have been willing to bet that his favorite way to spend an evening was to order a steak dinner and a bottle of booze from room service, and dine in front of the TV set, probably in his underwear. "Sorry," he said, "can't make it tomorrow. How about Sunday?"

"Fine," Lee said, pleased. "Four o'clock?"

"Okay, but maybe I better warn you," he said huskily. "I got an ulterior motive."

"Oh?" Lee said wearily. Farley just couldn't help himself.

"*I* think—" He leaned his head close to hers, enveloping her in Binaca and bourbon fumes. "*I* think maybe we could do a little business."

She frowned at him. "Business?"

"Well, you probably think this is a little tactless, I mean right after Kate's getting killed, but I'm not the kind of guy who beats around the bush. I'm the kind of guy who lays it on the table."

Before Farley laid it on the table it was apparently necessary to move her even farther into the corner and to loom over her more closely still, with his hand propped against the wall near her head in that possessive, vaguely suggestive way that she hated, that surely all women hated.

"What I'm talking about," he murmured through barely parted lips, "is that with Kate dead, I'm in a position to take on another property or two . . . and you could sure stand a little marketing, if you don't mind some friendly advice. You got yourself a lot of free publicity the last couple of days, and now's the time to take advantage of it." He paused. "Old Man Sawyer's gonna be looking for a new endorser for the Featherlite line now. With a little help from me you could be it."

"Thanks very much, Farley," she said, "but I'm not ready

for a manager yet." Or to be marketed on the strength of publicity from Kate's murder. And she was certainly not ready to be a "property" of Farley Stratton's.

He cocked his head. "There's big bucks out there, babe, that's what it's all about. Besides," he breathed, "it'd give us a chance to get to know each other better. You know, relate."

"Well, it's certainly tempting," Lee said, edging away along the wall, "but I think I'd better say no. Let me win a big tournament or two first so there's something to market."

"No, you got it backward. Let me explain the way it works."

She looked up at an ornate golden clock on a mantel. "Oh, gosh, is it that late already? I have to run. See you Sunday then, four o'clock."

"Right on, babe," he said, and sent her on her way with a moist kiss blown from the palm of a fleshy hand.

When she and Peg compared notes on the drive to the motel, there was only one piece of solid news between them, and that was Peg's.

"Somebody told me Wilma Snell went around with Kate on Wednesday morning, so I made sure to talk to her to see if she had anything interesting to say."

"And?"

"And she said some new kid was caddying for Kate. One of those college boys that were hanging around the parking lot looking for a bag. Anyway, the point is Ben wasn't caddying for her."

Lee frowned. "And he wasn't on the practice tee with her that night either. Still, that doesn't mean anything. He might have—"

"She fired him."

"*Fired* him! Why?"

Peg shook her head. "I don't know."

"When?"

"That morning. At least that was the impression Wilma had."

Lee stared out at the pallid, moonwashed sand dunes north

of the freeway. "In the morning she fires the man who's caddied for her for ten years . . ." she said slowly, ". . . and in the evening she's murdered."

"Very perceptive. Believe it or not, I made the same correlation myself." She glanced briefly at Lee. "I suppose," she said a little plaintively, "that the proper thing to do is to pass this on to the police too and let them be the ones to look into it."

"It is," Lee said firmly. "I'll do it tomorrow."

They were quiet as Peg swung the BMW off Highway 1 and took the Fremont Street off-ramp into Seaside. After a few blocks she turned into the Motel 6 parking lot and stopped the car, leaving the motor running gently.

"By the way," Lee said, as she opened the door, "I'm meeting Farley Stratton Sunday."

Peg blinked. "How'd you arrange that?"

"Oh, Farley's the kind who feels honor-bound to make a pass at any female he meets—"

"I've met him," Peg said stonily, "and he didn't make a pass at me, the crud."

"—and so we set something up. I may be imagining things, but I don't think Farley liked it when I brought up Kate's business affairs. I think there's something fishy there."

"I'll ask my contact to see what she can dig up." Peg switched off the engine. "Let's think about this a minute, Lee. We aren't playing games here. For all we know Farley really did kill Kate. We can't have you going off alone with him somewhere."

"Don't worry, there's no way I'd go off alone anywhere with Farley Stratton. I'm meeting him at Carmel Point after the round, in the Cormorant Room."

"I'll come with you."

"Somehow," Lee said, smiling, "I don't think that would work. Look, there's nothing to worry about. It'll be broad daylight. Very public."

"I don't know. . . ."

"And Farley may be a crook but even he wouldn't be crude enough to murder anyone in the Cormorant Room."

Peg's throaty laugh rumbled through the darkness.

"True," she said, and started up the motor again. "Well, get a good night's sleep. Tomorrow's the big day."

"Big day?"

Peg looked at her oddly. "The finals. Or did you forget?"

"I forgot," Lee said.

"You," Peg said severely, "have got to get your priorities in order."

9

At 2:30 A.M. Lee's priorities got themselves smartly in order. After two hours of restless sleep her eyelids flipped open on their own and she lay on her back, wide awake, staring at the dark ceiling and worrying about "the finals," as Peg had called them.

There were actually two competitions involved. The one Peg had been referring to was the pro-am final round, in which the teams of three amateurs and one professional would be playing for prizes and prestige. This contest was not a major source of worry to Lee, although for Peg's sake she hoped they'd do well. The amateur prizes ranged from trophies, to dinner sets, to sleeves of golf balls. The pros were competing as usual for money, but of a minor variety; first prize for the professional member of the winning foursome was $6,500, with amounts ranging sharply downward from there.

Sixty-five hundred dollars would, of course, have been highly welcome, but Lee's group had as much chance of making first place as they did of winning the gold medal in the luge at the Winter Olympics. With their record so far, if they won anything at all their prizes were likely to be dinner-for-two certificates for the amateurs and three or four hundred dollars for Lee. And while four hundred dollars was nothing to be sneezed at, it would cover no more than Lou's salary and the motel bill. She would still be thoroughly in the red for the week and deeper in the hole than ever.

It was the other competition that was keeping her awake—the professional cut to determine who would be battling it out for the major prize money. At the close of play tomorrow—or rather, later today—the pros' scores, tallied over all three rounds, would be added up. The top seventy or so would play in the pros-only final round on Sunday. The rest would pack up and move dispiritedly on to the next stop, Reno, hoping for better luck.

Lee hoped desperately not to be among them, and she thought she had a chance. Her fine one-below-par score of 71 in the second round had brought her total to 151; it wasn't a great two-round score, but she was in a lot better shape than she'd been in after the first day's horrible 80, particularly because some of her competitors had done as badly in the second round as she'd done in the first. If she could make par again in the third round, her probability of surviving the cut was good. And this cut really mattered. It was big-time money, the reason so many of the big-time players were there.

The total purse was $400,000. Fifteenth or twentieth place, where she could realistically (well, optimistically) hope to wind up given two more good days in a row, would bring something like $5,000. It wouldn't quite make her break even for the year, but it was close. More than that, it would give her the sense of success she desperately needed after a rookie season that had been so much tougher than she'd expected. And most important, it would make a lot of difference in the way the WPGL looked at her.

With only two weeks left to the official year (the post-September tournaments didn't count), she had no chance whatever of making the exempt list for the following season's tour no matter how well she did, but then she had never expected to, and that wasn't the issue. The issue was that her earnings record had been so miserable that the WPGL was more than likely to yank her tour card entirely—something she didn't want to think about—unless something good happened during these last few weeks of the season. And a

$5,000 prize at the Pacific-Western would certainly be something good. It would, she was sure, save her card.

She rolled over and looked at the glowing green face of her alarm clock. Three-fifteen. And she needed to be up at six to get in an hour's warm-up before teeing off. She tried to force herself back to sleep by breathing deeply and evenly, by clearing her mind, by relaxing her muscles one by one from the toes up, by imagining herself gliding like a seagull over a deserted shoreline, walking like a slow-motion figure in a peaceful forest, drifting like a jellyfish under the surface of a quiet, blue-green sea.

At four o'clock she got up and made herself a cup of hot chocolate, using water from the tap and a Swiss Miss packet that had been in a pocket of her suitcase as long as she could remember. She sat in the dark and rocked slowly back and forth, hugging herself while she drank the soothing, syrupy stuff. At 4:45 she went back to bed. At 5:10 she fell asleep again.

At 5:40 the telephone rang.

She groped for the receiver with her eyes glued shut. "Hello?" she mumbled, only half-awake. "What is it?"

The line was silent.

"Hello?" she said again.

She heard a long, hoarse breath drawn slowly in, then let slowly out. *Hunhh-hoooo.* A moist, strangling sound.

She was still flat on her back, but her eyes popped open. Something spidery seemed to crawl up the base of her neck and into her hair.

"Who is this?" she said.

"Lee Ofsted?" The voice was ragged, husky; a hoarse whisper.

"Who is this?" she repeated tensely.

"This is Ellis Sawyer. I'm calling from Baltimore." Again the long, rasping breath. *Hunhh-hoooo.*

Her mind spun. Ellis Sawyer? Milt's father, the head of Sawyer Sports Equipment? She blew out a sigh of relief, then felt abruptly foolish. Who had she thought it was? What exactly had she been afraid of?

"Did I wake you?" he asked.

"Mr. Sawyer, it's only a little after five in California, and I have to play today."

He chuckled. It was not an endearing sound; more a moist gargle than a laugh.

"I wanted to catch you before you played. I believe you're entered in the Reno Classic next week, isn't that so?" He paused for another labored breath. "I'll be making a rare business trip there myself, and I thought we might discuss a little business of our own. Let's say Tuesday, over lunch?"

She pushed herself up to a sitting position against the head of the bed, rubbing out of her eyes whatever sleep was left, trying to remember what she knew about Ellis Sawyer. He was a huge, dissipated-looking buffalo of a man, wide-hipped, broad-shouldered, and grossly overweight; she knew that from his pictures. And he was supposed to rule his empire with a remote but iron fist; she knew that too. He had won several celebrated and ruthless court battles, and he had ground numerous people who opposed him into pulp, including his son Milton. Not that she could imagine Milt opposing him. And now that she thought about it, she could remember Kate telling her something else about him, something odd, some personality quirk. . . .

"Are you there, Miss Ofsted?"

"I'm here," she said, trying to gather her wits. "What sort of business did you want to discuss?"

"The best kind. Financial business. I would like to offer you an endorsement contract for our products."

Lee sat up straighter, swinging her feet over the side of the bed. "Why?"

"I beg your pardon?"

"Why do you want to offer me an endorsement contract?"

There was a moment's silence before he spoke. "Well now, that's a different approach." He produced his ropy chuckle again and Lee shivered. "All right, I'll be frank with you, my dear."

There was another breath and a heavy rustling, and Lee imagined him settling back into a great leather chair in his office and lifting his massive, fleshy chins to the ceiling as he considered how to phrase his next words. "As you know, my dear, for some time Sawyer has had a mutually satisfactory arrangement with Kate O'Brian. Now that that relationship has been tragically terminated, we are looking for a replacement.''

''Why me?''

He chuckled again, with little more success at sounding avuncular. ''You make it sound like a death sentence, not a wonderful opportunity. All right, let me tell you why you. In the first place, you already use Sawyer Featherlites by choice, without remuneration. That's important. That's important to me.'' *Hunhh-hoooo.* ''It means integrity, you see.''

Lee didn't bother telling him that if Kate had been giving away a good set of Ping, or MacGregor, or Lynx clubs, she would have been happily using those right now, also without remuneration.

''Moreover,'' he went on slowly, ''we are interested in reaching the younger market, the club players. We have not been overly successful there, to be perfectly candid. I believe we would be wise to form an association with a young and rising player such as yourself, my dear.'' *Hunhh-hoooo.* There was more rustling in the background.

''And let us not forget,'' he added in a viscous, confidential whisper, ''that your very attractive appearance would provide a, mm, hmm, sexual allure that would be most valuable in our advertising.''

When Graham had said approximately the same thing, she had been pleased. When Sawyer said it she shuddered. She suddenly remembered what it was that Kate had told her about him. Kate had met him only once, in his office. She had found him at his desk, in an antique, high-backed leather chair from which he hadn't bothered to rise. Attached to the rear of the chair's back had been a thick roll of white butcher paper on a revolving drum. The paper had been pulled over the top of the chair so that it covered the back and Sawyer sat leaning against it. He hadn't remarked on it himself, but later Kate had mentioned it to someone else, who had told her that Sawyer couldn't bear having his skin touch soiled leather, and that every morning at eight and every afternoon at one-thirty a fresh section of butcher paper was pulled down for him.

The image had remained with Kate in an oddly unpleasant way, and it had stuck with Lee too.

"Thanks, Mr. Sawyer," she said, "but I don't think I'd be interested."

"I was thinking," he said blandly, "of something along the order of an initial two-year contract at ten thousand dollars a year."

That cleared her head of any remaining cobwebs. Ten thousand dollars for two years. Added to reasonable winnings, it would be enough to see her through two more tour seasons without the constant, chafing anxiety of money worries. Enough to let her take risks and go for the birdies and the big purses, instead of shooting for the fat, safe part of the green and the relatively sure but minuscule thirtieth- or fortieth-place prizes that didn't even cover expenses. And maybe with two years of worry-free golf she'd hit her stride and play the kind of game she knew was in her. Once she did that, her career would be made. It was really something to think about.

She thought about it for all of two seconds. "I don't think I'd be interested," she repeated, then took a breath and steamed ahead. "I think the reason you're offering me this is that I have a . . . a sensation value because everyone knows I found Kate's body, and some people might even think I . . . Well, I'm not interested."

Am I crazy? she thought. What would Peg say if she told her she'd just turned down a twenty-thousand-dollar contract? What would Cobe say? What would she herself have said if someone had told her a week ago that she was going to do it? But that was exactly the point. A week ago the world was different. A week ago Kate was alive and Sawyer wasn't interested in Lee Ofsted. And now that he was, she wasn't about to take advantage of Kate's murder, no matter what the reward. The thought made her skin crawl.

"Let's not jump to conclusions, my dear," Sawyer breathed. "We have been interested in you for some time now."

"You have?" If that was true, it was different. Her spirits lifted cautiously. "Mr. Sawyer, do you mean that when Milt was talking to me about a contract the other day he was serious?"

"Milton?" Sawyer spat out the name with incredulity and contempt, as if Lee had just asked if Milt wasn't the real brains behind the company. "Milton offered you a contract?"

"Well, no, not exactly. We were just—"

"I have no idea what he was talking about. Milton arranges the paperwork, the fine print, the details. *I* make the offers."

"Oh," she said, and glanced at the bedside clock. She was going to have to get moving. "Well, then—"

"Miss Ofsted, I want you on our team. There you are; I can't be any more frank than that, now can I?" There was more rustling. The butcher paper? "Now, what would it take to get you to join our team?"

"Mr. Sawyer, I simply don't—"

"Fifteen thousand annually?"

This was horrible. Turning down that kind of money was putting a serious strain on her principles. "I'm afraid not," she said briskly. "I would expect to be paid as much as you were paying Kate, no less."

That made her feel better, less naive. He had made a businesslike offer, she had made a businesslike counteroffer, and if he chose not to accept it, that was his affair. Case closed.

"That might be considered," he said. "In time."

If her heart didn't stop, it gave a convincing imitation. *A hundred and ten thousand dollars a year?* My God, how much strain could her principles bear? Out of frustration she jerked her head sharply. Who asked for this? She just didn't want to think about it, didn't want to accept the money, didn't want to turn it down and wonder for the rest of her life if she was being a short-sighted, narrow-minded boob.

"Mr. Sawyer, I have to be on the course in two hours. I simply can't—"

"We'll talk about it Tuesday. Shall we say noon, at the

Café Gigi in the MGM Grand? I prefer not to leave the hotel. Simply ask the *maître d'* for my table.''

"Well, no, I don't think so. I think we'd better just forget the whole—''

"Ah, and I'm having a new set of Featherlites prepared for you; I know your specifications. You should have them in time for the Classic. According to the newspapers, your three-wood is, mm, hmm, no longer usable. We can't have that, can we?''

"Mr. Sawyer—''

"And very good luck in your tournament, my dear.''

"Mr. Sawyer—''

Click.

10

"JESUS H. CHRIST!"

Startled by the outburst, Lee looked at Lou, who was staring down into her golf bag, the driver's green knit cover in his hand. With a grimace he flung the cover theatrically to the ground, shuddered mightily, and wiped his hand on his shapeless gray pants.

Lee sighed. Lou was a man of many parts, and his melodramatic moods were not her favorites. There were more appropriate ways, she thought, for him to express his opinion as to whatever it was that was annoying him now. Particularly inasmuch as they had only twenty minutes to tee-off; a heck of a time for him to upset her concentration.

"All right, Lou," she said mildly, "was there some point you wanted to make?"

"Yucch," he explained, continuing to stare at the clubs, his lips curled.

Lee sighed again and stepped out of her slot on the Cypress Point practice range, trying to calm her mounting irritation. He knew better than this, and she already had more than enough on her mind; that bizarre predawn call from Ellis Sawyer, for one thing.

"Lou," she said evenly, "I have worked my way up through all my other clubs and would dearly like a relaxed few minutes with the driver. Can't you just let me have—My God!''

She had been reaching for the driver herself, but now she froze too, hand outstretched, staring down at the upright clubs; at the driver, to be precise. The club head was heavily smeared with blood, thick and reddish brown, and just beginning to coagulate into horrible, gluey, hanging strands. There was no mistaking it. It had to be either blood or drying ketchup, and it didn't smell like ketchup. It smelled awful.

Her stomach turned over, and for a second she thought she might be sick, but revulsion quickly gave way to disorientation, a shivery sense of having been here before, of moving in slow, repeating circles that had been going on forever. The base of her spine prickled as acutely as if a fingernail had been drawn down it. Had there been *another* murder? Was another body lying right this minute in a pond? Was it going to be this way from now on? Every time she played, would she find a bloody . . .

Steady now.

She closed her eyes and made herself take a slow, even breath. With it her mind seemed to gather itself together and settle down. She opened her eyes, forcing herself to look dispassionately at the club. Someone was going to a lot of trouble on her account, first to frame her and now, apparently, to frighten her. For what could this be but a warning, an attempt to intimidate her, to make her back off and stop asking questions? Keep poking around, somebody was telling her in very unsubtle terms, and you're going to wind up with *your* head bashed in.

Well, they'd frightened her—for a few moments anyway—but they damn well hadn't intimidated her. If anything, they'd spurred her on, made her angry—as much by the repellent grossness of this new ploy as by anything else. (Although why she should expect sensitivity and taste from Kate's murderer she didn't know.) Besides, if they were going to this revolting length to make her back off, then she must be getting somewhere, even if it didn't seem that way, and she wasn't about to quit now. Not a chance.

"What's it supposed to be?" Lou asked angrily. "A joke?"

"I suppose so, but not too funny, is it? Lou, how could this happen? I thought you were taking care of the clubs last night? Didn't you have them with you?"

"Sure, I did. . . . Well, not exactly."

She waited.

"I mean, I cleaned them up after yesterday and then I left them in the bag room overnight. That's what all the caddies do."

She nodded. It was what all the caddies did, all right, which meant that people had been in and out of the bag room until midnight and beyond, going to and from the nearby lighted driving ranges. There was a kid who served as an attendant, but Lee knew from experience that things were usually pretty lax. It would have been child's play for someone to get at her clubs.

"How was I supposed to know," Lou asked defensively, "that some weirdo was gonna—"

"It's okay, Lou. It wasn't your fault. Will you put the cover back on and give it to one of the marshals? Ask him to call Lieutenant Sheldon and tell him I found it in my bag."

"And what are we gonna use to drive?"

"We'll work it out."

"Like how?"

"I'll use the three-wood the pro lent me. How else?"

"A *borrowed* three instead of a driver?" She hadn't known his voice could go that high. "Come on, Lee, how the hell do you expect to get around eighteen tough holes—"

"Lou," she said tightly, "don't do this to me! I have enough problems!" The squeaky rise of her own voice startled her, and she could feel the cords standing out in her throat. Maybe she wasn't as brave as she imagined. Indignant, yes, but scared too. Oddly, knowing that made her angrier still. If this wretched killer thought he could frighten her at will and ruin her life like this, he had another thing coming.

She had never before spoken to Lou like that, and it made his jaw drop.

"Lou," she said more kindly, "you know distance is my strong suit. I can make two-twenty with a three-wood. And this isn't a terrifically long course where you need an overpowering drive; just sixty-five hundred yards. We'll do all right."

Lou continued to scowl at her for a few seconds, then abruptly turned his toothy, twisty grin on her. "Right," he said cheerfully, and bent to pick up the head cover. "Right you are. No big deal. Back in a minute."

Uh-oh. When Lou smiled so that his strong, crooked teeth seemed to stick straight out at you and you could see his brown gums, that meant he was worried about your game, and when Lou was worried about your game, he generally turned out to be right.

But he trotted obediently with the covered club to a marshal, who took it, listened to him with an impatient nod, and then made an annoyed, easy-to-read motion with his hand: *It's your starting time. Get on with it, will you?*

Lou came back, his monkeyish face still slashed by a rubbery grin. "We'll do fine. Who needs a driver? We use the three-wood the pro lent us, right? So we lose a few yards distance, we make it up hitting right down the line. Right?"

"Right," she said, and laughed. The hype was a bad sign, but at least it was "we" and not "you." That meant he still had some confidence left.

With good reason. She bore down with a curiously intense single-mindedness, unbothered by the gusty, on-again-off-again rain that squalled unseasonably over the course in brief, cold bursts. She birdied the first hole and parred the next four, then bogied on the 522-yard sixth, but came right back with two more birdies. Then she parred the next six in a row. She was playing marvelously (all right, amazingly); two under par after fourteen, without a genuinely bad shot all day. And all without a driver.

Sam Snead liked to talk about the benefits of playing "cool-mad," this term for a state of controlled tension, and for the first time she understood what he meant. She plucked her ball out of the cup at fourteen and waved to an applauding crowd. Maybe she ought to ask Lou to smear some blood on her driver every day.

Not funny. She focused on her game again and scored yet another birdie at the short fifteenth, on an arcing, downhill ten-yard putt that brought a rousing cheer from the drenched gallery. Peg grinned at her and lifted her putter in salute. Lee hadn't yet passed on the news about the bloodied driver. The moment she heard about it, it would be the end of Peg's ability to concentrate on golf. And Lee's too, very likely. She smiled blandly back at Peg and headed for the sixteenth.

The sixteenth at Cypress Point. Certainly the most famous, most photographed, and most gloriously beautiful hole of golf in the world. And the most terrifying, which took some doing for a measly 233-yard par-three affair. To begin with, the green was surrounded by big beds of pulpy, grubby iceplant—the most frustrating kind of rough imaginable. That was to begin with, and if that was all there was, it would have been just one more tricky three-wood, not the heebie-jeebie-inducing fortitude-destroyer that it was.

The thing was, in order to get to that iceplant-locked green, you had to stand on one rocky, wind-scoured peninsula and hit the ball onto another. And you had to do it across 200 yards of choppy Pacific Ocean. Either that or go the "safe" way, a 125-yard carry over the edge of the surf to the wide saddle of the far promontory. From there it was a chip to the green and, with luck, one or two putts. Birdies were impossible that way, except by out-and-out luck, and bogeys were frequent. Worse, if you took this less blood-curdling route, you had to bear the sneering contempt of scornful galleries and disdainful fellow players.

As a result, most golfers went over the water, directly for the green and for glory. Few achieved either. In the third round of the 1953 Crosby, Porky Oliver had taken a memorable sixteen strokes on this hole, and hundreds of ordinarily competent golfers had driven five, six, or seven balls in a row directly into the waves, or bounced them off the opposite cliff, which amounted to the same thing.

The fans, of course, loved it. And here on this gray and miserable fall day, at the wettest, most blustery place on the course, the biggest, happiest gallery of all had gathered, tricked out in parkas, sou'westers, and mackintoshes, mukluks, Wellingtons, and hip waders, to watch the golfers make fools of themselves.

As usual, the golfers had obliged and things had slowed down; four groups were stacked up waiting. Lee's amateur partners slipped on jackets or waterproofs and went looking for what shelter they could find, but Lee stayed to watch, joining Lou in the lee of a gale-warped cypress, where they made a shared seat of her bag in the time-honored fashion, pro perched on the supported top end and caddie hunkered down on the bottom.

The weather didn't bother her. For one thing, the damp, bracing air reminded her of Portland, Oregon, her hometown. For another, she'd learned to play golf under conditions as bad as these, at Hahn Air Force Base, not far from the small army supply depot she'd been stationed at in Germany. The base sat on top of a desolate ridge that the Germans wryly called the Hunsrück, which meant "dog's back," and it drew rain, fog, and wind the way its namesake drew fleas. As a result, she was accustomed to playing golf in weather that purpled her ears and made her eyes water, on fairways that could have passed for swamps, and on greens so slow you could manicure your nails while waiting for your ball to roll into the hole.

The F-16s that had shrieked ear-shatteringly from the adjacent runways had been character-builders too. Lee had learned not to be one of those people who "missed short putts because of the uproar of butterflies in the adjacent meadow," as P. G. Wodehouse had put it so memorably.

"Look," Lou said. "Kendall's going to go for it."

Lee craned her neck to get an unobstructed view of

Dorothy Kendall, two groups ahead of her, lining up for her tee-shot, then bouncing the ball off the cliff and into the sea. The next ball did the same. The crowd stirred happily. Those who think that all the bloodthirsty sports fans can be found at automobile racing, or boxing, or bullfighting would find a visit to the gallery at Cypress Point's sixteenth hole enlightening.

By the same token, Lee too derived a highly unsporting satisfaction from watching her competitor flail away, not that she'd admit it to Lou. On her third try, Dorothy finally made it across—and into the iceplant—and stomped angrily off.

Beside Lee, Lou cackled happily. "Five strokes, counting penalties. Everybody's blowing it out there. You know what? We're gonna make the cut and make it good."

"So far, so good," Lee agreed. "But I think I'd better play it safe on this one. Even if I bogey, I'll still be two under with two to go."

"No way," Lou said, shocked. "We gotta go for it, Lee. We've been bopping beauts into the wind all day."

Bopping beauts. She turned toward him, frowning. Those had been almost the first words Kate had spoken to her that day at Bent Tree, and Lee had heard her use the phrase several times since. But never anyone else—except Lou.

"Lou," she said slowly, "did you ever pack a bag for Kate?"

He pulled the frazzled remnants of a Kleenex out of his pocket and dabbed at his reddening nose. "A couple of times—maybe three. Long ago, before Mr. Ben got her."

"Why didn't you ever tell me?"

"Why'n't you ever ask me?" he answered naturally enough.

"How come it was only a couple of times?"

He shrugged. "She was a pain in the ass. It wasn't worth it."

"How do you mean, a pain?"

"A pain. Hairtrigger temper. Everything had to be just right, her way. Chew you out right in front of the galleries.

Right on national TV." He tucked the shreds of tissue back into his pocket. "Ben was welcome to her."

"Lou, do you know where Ben is?"

He looked sidewise at her. "What do you want Ben for?"

"I heard a rumor that Kate fired him. I wanted to find out if it was true."

"Why? What's it matter?" Lou wasn't trying to be rude, as far as she could tell. This was the way he communicated. "You think he killed her because she canned him? Sort of like the butler did it?"

"I don't know, Lou," she said honestly. "I really don't."

"Me neither," he said with finality. "What the hell." His tone, when he was forced to talk for very long about anything besides golf was generally bored. It was bored now.

He grunted and stood up. "We better loosen up. We're next."

Lee stood up too and abstractedly did a few limbering twists from the hips.

"So," he said, "we gonna go for the green or not?"

Lou was old for a touring caddie, probably nearing sixty, and he had more than his share of irritating idiosyncrasies: He was glum most of the time, bossy all of it, and by turns patronizing and imperious—all of which explained why he'd never established a long-term relationship with a golfer. But he knew what he was doing, he seemed to have confidence in Lee, and he got the best out of her. And what little he said was generally right.

"Why not?" She grinned. "What the hell."

"Right on," he said, and jerked the bag over his shoulder. "Let's go for it."

They went for it and they got it, and when Lee walked off the eighteenth green forty minutes later she did it on a six-inch cloud. She had finished with a two-under-par 70, not only good enough to make the cut, but good enough to put her in twentieth place for the moment with a three-day score of five over par and a lot of momentum going for her. She had picked up a gallery of a hundred or so after the sixteenth, and they had cheered her when she sank the last seven-foot putt. Someone actually asked for her autograph, and three kids had scrambled to get her ball.

This, she thought happily, is what it's supposed to be like, what it would be like most of the time once she really found her game. Up in the ABC television tower, in front of the still-hooded camera (one good showing hadn't earned her *Wide World of Sports* coverage), a technician smiled and made a circle of thumb and forefinger: A-OK. In the first row of the grandstand, Nick Pittman and Farley Stratton also mimed signs of approval and encouragement.

And Milt Sawyer jogged floppily up to pump her hand. "They showed what you did on sixteen on closed-circuit. It was fantastic. Everybody went wild. Gosh, I'm glad you took my advice on that take-away."

"Why, thank you, Milt. If not for Lou I'd never have tried it." She almost smiled at herself. What a pleasant role, and how easy it was to fall into it. Lee Ofsted, gracious, self-effacing star, comfortably at home with the adulation of the masses, generously giving credit where due.

"You know," Milt said, "I was having a quiet dinner with Jackie last year at The Nest in Indian Wells—You know the Nest?—and Jackie said that on a windy day that is the most difficult hole in America."

"Jackie?"

He frowned at her. "Nicklaus."

"Oh, Jackie Nicklaus. Well, thanks again, Milt. I really appreciate it." She made a move to walk on. "I think I'd better turn in my scorecard."

"Wait, Lee. Just hold up for a second, can't you?"

She waited.

Milt grinned as broadly as his sun-cracked lips would allow. "I hear you heard from the Founder."

"The Founder?"

"My father."

"Oh. Yes."

"I told you we were interested in you, didn't I? Well, I guess you know that my father follows my advice on these matters, and he agrees with me completely. You'd be just great for Sawyer, and Sawyer would be just great for you.

You know, he was thinking about Nancy or Kathy, but I told him we needed some new blood on the way up, and we couldn't do any better than you."

"Thanks very much, Milt, but to tell the truth, I honestly don't think—"

"I talked to him a couple of hours ago, and, boy, was he impressed with you."

"If he was impressed, it was because I told him I wouldn't settle for anything less than Kate was getting."

"You *told* him that?" Milt's round eyes bugged. "I don't know, Lee, that's not the way he likes to do business. He's used to calling the shots. You actually gave him a figure?"

"Well, no, I didn't name a figure, but he knows what it's going to be: a hundred and ten thousand dollars." She set her lips, trying not to feel ridiculous. What was she doing demanding an obscene amount of money, more than she'd earned in any five years put together just for saying "Does Lee Ofsted use Sawyer Featherlites? Just ask me, honey" a few dozen times. She sighed, wishing she had been more firm with Ellis Sawyer in the first place. But at five-forty in the morning who was clear-headed?

From Milt's stricken look, it might have been his own pocket the money was coming from. "A hundred and ten thousand . . . I don't know, Lee." He shifted, pawing the grass with a stubby toe, and lowered his voice. "You know, my father's a little funny to work with. He won't negotiate. He makes an offer, and that's that. If you start trying to deal, it's all over. That's what happened to Dottie. She started making demands." He spread his hands, palms up. "Pop dropped her like a hot brick and went out and signed Kate the next day. Literally. The next day."

"Dottie? Do you mean Dorothy Kendall? Was she with Sawyer before Kate?"

"Sure, didn't you know that?"

"No. When?"

"Up until last year. Kate was only with us for . . . oh,

fourteen months. Before then, we had Dottie for over seven years." He looked at her peculiarly. "Why?"

"No particular reason." No reason other than that it gave the vitriolic Dorothy Kendall one more reason to hate Kate's guts.

"Lee, take my advice. Let *him* make the offer. You just take the money and run. Look, he listens to me. I think I can get him to put out thirty-five, forty thousand. Push him for more than that and you'll just be throwing it away. Let me tell you what Fuzzy said to me about endorsements last year. We were playing a round after the Open—Fuzzy, Calvin, and me—and Fuzzy—"

"No," she interrupted, shaking her head. "I don't like negotiating either. My fee is a hundred and ten thousand and that's exactly what I intend to tell him."

Milt made a choking sound. *"Why?"*

Even if she'd known the answer to that, there wasn't time to tell him. She was overdue at the scoring tent. "Milt, they're waiting for me. I better go sign my card."

"Have you been getting advice from Farley Stratton?" he called after her. "Did I ever tell you what JoAnne said about Farley? We were having drinks at The Well—I mean JoAnne and me . . ."

At the scoring tent she had to pass a scowling Dorothy Kendall on the way out. Dorothy had wound up with 81 and was almost certainly out of the tournament.

Lee hesitated, then spoke. "Sorry about your rotten luck on the sixteenth," she said tentatively, knowing it was a mistake. But she really meant it in a way; she was trying to make amends for that brief, uncharacteristic surge of glee while watching Dorothy haplessly whack balls into the waves.

Dorothy didn't answer. She merely glared at her, her tight face clenched and sullen, and waited for Lee to get out of her way.

Even after she left, the afterimage of the older golfer's hot stare seemed to keep burning through her. *Why, she really, truly is capable of killing someone,* Lee thought, and for the first time she genuinely believed it, deep in her bones.

Inside the little tent Lee sat down with her partners at a folding table covered with a red cloth, and the four of them went over their cards carefully, signed them, and gave them to an impassive official. Everybody was feeling good. With a best-ball foursome score of 60 for the round, they would certainly share in the awards.

On her way out she met Wilma Snell, the boxy, aging rabbit who had moved up to take Kate's slot. Wilma, in the following foursome, had had a good day too and was close behind Lee, tied for twenty-first place. Lee exchanged a grin and a thumbs-up sign with her and walked on feeling even better. She was rooting for the taciturn, melancholy Wilma to do well; a decent showing on Sunday would very likely put her back in the exempt class next season, where she wouldn't have to scramble every Monday with kids young enough to be her daughters.

She had to skirt the eighteenth green again to get to the clubhouse, and there was Graham Sheldon, waiting for her on the edge of the crowd.

She smiled, pleased to see him. "This is beginning to be a habit."

"It's all part of our friendly service. You keep pulling blood-covered clubs out of your bag, I'll keep waiting for you at the eighteenth green. Note how much I'm learning about golf, by the way. I know how many greens there are. I know what a green is, for that matter."

"Amazing."

He looked at her for a moment, his head cocked. "You're all right?" he asked quietly.

"All right?" For a moment she didn't know what he was talking about. "That stupid club, you mean?" She dismissed it with a shrug. "Lieutenant, I broke par! I actually birdied the sixteenth, can you imagine? I was so excited I turned around and double-bogeyed the seventeenth, but on the—"

"Whoa. Birdies, double bogeys . . . We're getting pretty technical here."

"Well, a birdie—" She stopped with a sigh. "In answer to your question, yes, I'm fine. That business with the club didn't bother me at all. It just made me mad. Did you find out anything from it? Was it supposed to be a warning, or what?"

"Oh, I think we can pretty safely assume it was a warning. We'll get to that later. Let's go someplace we can talk."

"Fine. Do I get hot dogs again? I'm starving. I didn't even have a chance for a doughnut after the front nine."

He smiled, took her arm, and steered her through the crowd towards the clubhouse. "I'll do better than hot dogs. Why don't you take a shower and change? I'll wait for you here."

"A shower! Wow, this must be pretty fancy."

11

IT WASN'T FANCY, but it was a big step up from hot dogs. Graham drove her to Monterey, to the bustling, funky wharf, where fish markets, curio shops, restaurants, and seafood-cocktail stands lined up side by side atop the old pilings, and shiny black seals panhandled from the still, clear water below. They parked in the big lot at the foot of Washington Street and walked almost to the end of the wharf, to Abalonetti's, a noisy, congenial place full of the smell of garlic and seafood, with the feel of a friendly neighbor-lady's kitchen.

Lee began to order the Dover sole, but Graham interrupted magisterially. "Dover sole? You come to Monterey, to Fisherman's Wharf, and you order Dover sole?"

"But I like Dover sole."

"Have you ever had cioppino?"

She shook her head.

"Dover sole is just fish," Graham said with contempt. "You can get it anywhere. But you get the best cioppino in the world right here, right in Abalonetti's. It's an undisputed fact."

"He's right, honey," the waitress said kindly.

"Of course I am. We'll have the crab cioppino," Graham said to the waitress. "With plenty of squid. And a small carafe of white wine."

"Squid?" Lee said doubtfully. "I don't know about—"

"It's terrific," Graham said. "Like chicken, only better."

"Why is it," Lee mused, "that every time someone wants you to eat something disgusting he tells you it tastes like chicken? Rattlesnake, brains, eels, squid—"

"Trust me," Graham said, and closed his menu with a snap.

"Trust him, honey," the waitress said, and left with both menus.

Lee leaned back and sighed with pleasure. It was just the sort of place she liked, the sort of place she imagined when she thought of Monterey. And if she'd had time to think about such things over the last year or two, Graham Sheldon would have been just the sort of man she'd have imagined with her. He was in the leather-elbowed tweed jacket he'd worn the other day, but this time with a thick turtleneck sweater, and she would have been surprised if he didn't know how healthily attractive he looked, with his reddish hair mussed just enough by the breeze to add to the rugged, outdoorsy look he had anyway.

Or maybe he didn't know after all. His mind certainly seemed to be on other things. "How," he asked her over the salads, "is the investigation going?"

She glanced up. "The . . . ?"

"Investigation. Yours and Peg's. Your interrogation of everybody you could reach at the party last night."

"I wasn't *interrogating* them," she said uncomfortably. How did he find out these things anyway? "You can't just stand there at a cocktail party. You have to talk to people about something."

This earned the look it deserved. "Such as their relationship to Kate?"

"I didn't . . . Lieutenant, how do you know what I was talking to people about? Are you keeping tabs on me?"

"You better believe it."

"Why?"

But he didn't answer. "You promised me you wouldn't poke around at the party."

"I promised you I'd eat canapés and drink champagne. And I did."

He set down a glass of ice water hard. "Just what the hell do you think this is? A game? A joke? Are you playing at it?"

"No," she said, annoyed. "I'm not playing at it." Out of the corner of her eye she saw some heads turn, and she lowered her voice. "Kate was my friend, in case you forgot. That matters. And half the golf world probably believes I killed her by now. That matters too."

"And you don't think I'm capable of handling things without your help, is that it?"

Were his feelings hurt? Was he angry? It was hard to say. He wasn't too pleased about it, that was for sure, but she decided she might as well say what she felt. "What I think is that you're at a disadvantage because you don't understand golf—"

He cut her off abruptly. "And if I was investigating the murder of a nuclear scientist, would I have to know how to make atomic bombs? If it was a . . . a snake charmer, would I—" He made an impatient movement with his fork. "The hell with it. I'm tired of explaining it to people. You know what I mean."

"I just think you're liable to miss some nuances, that's all."

He lifted his eyebrows and widened his eyes. "Oh, *nuances*. . . ."

And with that, for no reason she could think of, they both began to laugh, so long and hard that she had to wipe her eyes. "Oh, dear. . . ."

The waitress returned with paper bibs to tie around their necks. "You have to forget about manners when you eat cioppino, honey," she said. "We're talking world-class messy here."

Then the cioppino itself came: huge bowls of pungent fish-and-tomato stew with clams, shrimp, and chunks of crab, all in their shells, sticking helter-skelter out of it. She followed the lead of people at other tables and sucked a white piece of crabmeat noisily out of its shell, tossed the splintered red shell into a big bowl in the center of their table and wiped tomato sauce and olive oil from her fingers. It was, she quickly discovered, a gratifyingly sensuous and primitive meal.

"Yum," she said. "Which pieces are the squid?"

He speared a white oval from her bowl for her. "These. The little rings."

She ate it from his fork, feeling intimate and daring. "Not bad, Lieutenant. Like chicken, only chewier."

"Good, I like a woman with an open mind. But does it strike you as a little peculiar to address someone whose fork you've just shared as 'lieutenant'?"

"A little."

"Then I have a suggestion. Why don't you call me 'Graham' and I'll call you 'Lee'? Would that be okay?"

That would be very okay. Long overdue, in fact. She had been thinking of him as "Graham" for some time now. She held his gaze for a few moments, happy and excited, and on the edge of something good, then thought she'd better get back to her seafood.

And Graham got back to business. "Lee, I want you to tell me about everything you've been doing: everyone you've been talking to, everything they said, every idea you've been hatching."

"All right." She was ready to tell him. Now that the golf round was over and her adrenaline was back to normal, that bloody driver in her bag had begun to skulk nastily at the back of her mind. No, she certainly didn't see it as a joke, and she was more than willing to admit that she was in over her head.

She began with some embarrassment, but he listened carefully and kindly, not interrupting except to ask questions, and she gained confidence as she spoke. By the time she'd finished, the bowl in the center was filled to the rim with shell fragments and the cioppino was down to its dregs. She put her spoon down and waited uneasily for his reaction.

"Well," he said slowly, while they rinsed their fingers in bowls of lemon water and dried them on fresh napkins the waitress delivered with their coffees, "you've told me a few things I didn't know about."

"Like what?"

"Like Kate firing her caddie. That might be important. You wouldn't know where to reach him?"

She shook her head. "I'll let you know if I hear. What else did I tell you that you didn't know? You said 'things.' "

"Don't be so literal; it's just a figure of speech. But I have to admit that your instincts are good. Almost everyone you've been wondering about, I've been wondering about too."

"Really?" she chirped, hugely pleased.

"Really."

"Well . . . who do *you* think did it?"

"It's a little early for that,"—he laughed—"but there are two people who are going to be getting a lot of my attention."

"Let me guess. Is Gilbert O'Brian one of them?"

He was transparently surprised. "How did you know that?"

"What don't you like about him?" she responded, question to question.

"It's hard to say, exactly." Holding his coffee in both hands, he watched a seagull stumble to a clumsy landing on a post outside the window and then pretend that it had been there all along. "There's something . . . glib about him, something just a little too casual, too confident—What's so funny?"

"You. I think you don't like him because he's too good-looking."

"Too—!" The cup banged into its saucer. "Now what the hell is that supposed to mean? That I'd try to hang a murder rap on him because he looks like Captain America?"

"No, of course not. It's just that men don't trust other men who are too handsome. Women are the same way. It's because of a perfectly natural sexual insecurity. Don't worry, I'm sure you won't let it influence you."

"Very kind of you," he grumbled, then after a moment: "Did you really think O'Brian was all that handsome?"

"He wasn't all that bad," Lee said with a smile. "If you happen to like the type. Now, who's the other person?"

"Kate's manager, Farley Stratton. Would you care to give me a Freudian analysis on why I don't like *him*?"

"Uh . . . no, I'm sure you have good reasons," she said carefully. The one piece of pertinent information she had neglected to tell him about earlier was her upcoming meeting with Farley. Graham, she was sure, would have forbidden it, and she would not have reacted kindly to being forbidden, and there would have been a quarrel. And she didn't want a quarrel.

"Oh, I don't know that I'm onto anything very solid," he said, mollified, "but I'd be willing to bet the guy was swindling her, and I'm damn sure going to find out how." He grinned suddenly. "Or maybe I just don't trust men who are too ugly?"

Sensibly, she held her peace, more excited than ever about meeting Farley. There was no doubt in her mind that she could get more out of him than Graham could, but it was going to take some planning. Telling Graham about it later on was also going to take some planning.

"All right," he said, "now can we consider that the official responsibility for this investigation has been passed from you to me? Will you keep out of it from now on?"

"You bet," she said earnestly. "It's your baby. I've retired from police work as of this minute."

"Peg too," he said. It wasn't a question.

"I'll pass the word."

Satisfied and relaxed, they sipped their coffee for a minute or two in silence. "What did you mean, 'almost everyone'?" Lee asked. "Who's on my list that isn't on yours?"

"I thought you just retired."

"Just interested, that's all."

"I see. Well, all right, I think we can rule Dorothy Kendall out."

"Dorothy?" Lee repeated, surprised. "But I just told you, not only did she lose a twelfth-place finish at Bent Tree because of Kate, she lost her endorsement contract to her too. I'm not accusing her of murder, but I don't see how you can rule her out. She's really a bitter person, full of—"

She stopped. Graham was smiling superiorly at her, slowly shaking his head back and forth.

"Nope," he said. "She's left-handed."

"So what?"

"Kate was struck on the left side of the head. From in front, according to the lab." When Lee didn't respond he went on. "To a clever detective like myself, the implication is inescapable: The blow was struck with the right hand."

Lee hesitated. "Uh-oh," she said. "I think maybe you really do need my help. You see—"

"Here we go again," he muttered, but he was still in a smug good humor.

"—almost every left-handed pro plays golf right-handed. That includes Dorothy."

That, she thought with satisfaction, had gotten his attention. He sat up straight and put down his cup in mid-swallow. "Why?" he asked suspiciously.

"Partly because most courses are laid out for a right-handed game, but also because the driving forces in the golf swing are the leading hip and arm, and . . . Look, just take my word for it. Dorothy plays right-handed."

He considered this soberly. "How was I supposed to know that?"

"That's the point I keep trying to make," she said exasperatedly. "There are lots of things you couldn't be expected to know, and you're not going to find them in police manuals."

"All right, let's say this left-handed business is true—"

"It is true."

"But would the left-hand-right-hand switch hold for hitting someone over the head with a golf club?"

"How would I know something like that?" she said, unable to keep from laughing. "It's not one of your standard shots."

"Ah, then we're even." He drained his coffee. "Neither one of us knows. I'll have to find out."

"But it's something that wouldn't have occurred to you to even think about—only a golfer would know. That's all I'm trying to say."

Frowning, Graham wiped his lips with a napkin, folded it, and placed it neatly beside his saucer. "I think," he said gravely, "that you have a point. You're right. I could use some technical know-how."

She put her own cup down. "Does that actually mean you want me to—"

"I don't want you to do anything," he said hurriedly. "I won't have any trouble lining up a consultant. God knows you can't walk five feet in Carmel without bumping into a golfer."

"But why couldn't *I* be a sort of consultant to you?"

"Because, one, you're personally involved, which is a no-no. Two, I want you to concentrate on your golf and knock 'em dead tomorrow, and leave the police work to me. Do *I* give *you* advice on how to drive a hit?"

"That's hit a drive."

"Well, there you are. And— What am I up to?"

"Three."

"Thank you. Three, you're only going to be here a couple of days more, and this case is going to take a lot longer than that." For a long moment he stared down at his empty coffee cup, rotating it slowly in his strong, long-fingered hands. Then he looked up soberly. "That's true, isn't it?" he asked quietly. "You're leaving Monday?"

"I have to. I need to get familiar with the course." If she'd been asked, she couldn't have said how she felt at that moment under his lucid, steady gaze. She could feel her heart thumping, she knew that. "I . . . I do have a two-day tournament in San Jose in a few weeks. I could always hop a bus and visit Carmel, I suppose."

"Would you?"

She hesitated. It had been a long time since she'd been willing to make even that much of a commitment. For a long time now golf had used up all of her energy, all of her mind. "Yes," she said.

"Good. But I'll come and pick you up instead." He leaned back in his chair and smiled at her. "Well," he said.

"Well," she said.

When they left the restaurant they bought a white paper sack of salt-water taffy at a cart with an umbrella and munched while they strolled back toward the car. A little sunshine was slipping through breaks in the dark clouds now, and the wind had disappeared almost completely. At the foot of the wharf they paused to watch a hurdy-gurdy man and his monkey. The man wore a straw boater and a striped jacket; the monkey was dressed like a bellhop. On a long leash the monkey went around the circle of watchers, irritatedly accepting pennies, stuffing them in a purselike pocket, and lifting its cap, letting the elastic band snap it back onto its head.

"So tell me," Lee said. "When do I get to hear what you've been doing about that bloody driver? Are your men out hunting for suspicious-looking people wearing Band-Aids?"

"Even as we speak. Only it's suspicious-looking chickens they're looking for."

"Funny, I almost thought you said chickens."

"I did."

"You mean that was chicken blood?"

"I do."

"Has it struck you," she said, thoughtfully unwrapping the waxed-paper on a piece of chocolate taffy, "that there seem to be an awful lot of birds involved in this case?"

When the monkey got up to them, Lee found a nickel and held it out. The monkey chittered briefly, ill-humoredly snatched the coin, bit it, and dropped it into its pocket. Then it quickly shook hands with her, the ends of its strange, dry fingers brushing her palm. It moved on to Graham, went through the same routine, and continued around the circle.

The hurdy-gurdy man stopped cranking and poured the coins into a wooden box. Then he gave the monkey a tin mug of water and something to eat from a small metal case. The monkey ate a few handfuls greedily, looking anxiously over its shoulder at the crowd.

"What's it eating, mister?" a little girl asked.

"Shrimp," the man said. "That's all it eats. Bay shrimp."

"Boy," somebody called out. "You got a job for another monkey?"

"Lee," Graham said as they headed toward the parking lot, "the lab says the blood was put on the club three to five hours before they ran their tests, which they did at eleven-thirty A.M."

"And Lou found it just before I teed off at eight-thirty, but I had my clubs right with me in plain sight from seven-thirty on—"

"Which means it had to have been done between six-thirty and seven-thirty this morning."

She nodded. "Right. Gee, police work is pretty simple when you get down to it. And now you want to know where my clubs were between six-thirty and seven-thirty."

"Exactly."

"I'm afraid this isn't going to be much help. . . ."

He waited, chin tucked in, eyebrows lifted.

"I don't think you're going to like this," she said, "but they were in the bag room all night. In an open rack."

"*Another* open rack?"

"Well, everybody uses the bag room, Graham," she said uncomfortably. "This isn't the sort of thing you expect to happen, you know."

"Mm. And I suppose hundreds of people had access to it."

"Millions. You're supposed to show a tag to get your bag, but at that time of the morning it's swamped with people taking them out and putting them in, and everybody's in a hurry. And the attendant is a local college kid who wouldn't know the ropes, or people's faces either. Anybody who looked like he knew what he was doing could have gotten hold of my bag."

"Terrific," Graham said. "Wonderful. All right, when you picked up the bag, can you remember if it was just the way you left it last night? Same position? Clubs in the same order?"

"I don't know. Lou picked it up, not me. He put it there last night too."

They had reached the dark-blue Plymouth now, and Graham looked at her across the roof as he unlocked the door. "How well do you know Lou?" he asked offhandedly.

"Lou? *Lou?* You've got to be kidding."

"How long has he been caddying for you?"

"Well, actually, only two or three times."

"He's not your regular caddie?"

She laughed. Rabbits didn't have regular caddies. Only the Chosen Ninety in the exempt class did. If you never knew until the Monday qualifying round whether or not you'd be playing in that week's tournament, how could you line up a permanent caddie? She explained this while she slid in and buckled on her seat belt. "So it's true that I don't know him very well, but the thought of him murdering Kate is . . . Why would he want to, anyway?"

"One thing at a time. We're talking about the clubs now, not Kate. They've been tampered with twice—in their bag—and who had a better opportunity to do that, or to turn a blind eye while somebody else did it, than your caddie? It would have been easy enough, wouldn't it?"

"Well, yes, I guess so, but . . ." She took some time to consider it, trying to be objective, but it wasn't any less absurd after a minute's thought, and she told him so. Firmly. Not Lou. Impossible.

"I've already asked him to caddy for me next week in Reno," she said, as if that proved something.

"I thought you couldn't arrange for a caddie in advance."

"But if you make the cut in a tournament you're exempt for the next one."

"Exempt?"

"You're automatically in. No Monday qualifying. So I *know* I'll need a caddie. Graham, it wasn't Lou."

"You're probably right," he said easily, and smiled at her. But she knew Lou was in for an interview in the near future, which he wouldn't care for in the least. That would be an interesting session: the irresistible force (Graham) against the immovable object (Lou). Her money was on Graham, but she imagined they'd both come out of it licking their wounds.

Graham started up the engine. "Where to?"

Lee glanced at her watch. "It's almost one-thirty. I'm supposed to give Peg some tips on pitching on the Pebble Beach practice green at two."

"Fine. We'll swing up to Ocean Boulevard and come down the drive from the north."

"Isn't that the long way?"

"Uh-huh, but it's the pretty way. You'll only be a little late."

They were well along the Seventeen-Mile Drive, past Point Joe, when she said, "Graham, there's something I forgot to tell you. I got a call from Ellis Sawyer this morning."

"The head of the firm?"

"Yes. He wants me to take Kate's place endorsing their products."

"And are you going to?"

"Well, I seem to be a little . . . ambivalent. I think I need some help deciding."

He pulled the car into a parking area overlooking a tiny, isolated beach strewn with smooth black pebbles and sea-worn driftwood and turned off the ignition.

"Now," he said, turning toward her and leaning an elbow on the steering wheel, "what's the problem?"

"The problem is, he offered me ten thousand a year to do it. The minute I hesitated he upped it to fifteen."

He looked at her without speaking for a moment. "That's a tough problem, all right."

"No, the thing is, I'm not worth it. Not for my golfing; not yet, anyway. He gave me a bunch of reasons, but I think he sees a . . . a ghoulish kind of publicity value in me, because I'm linked with Kate's murder." She rolled down her window. The fresh, fragrant sea air rolled in, as moist as fog.

"I'd feel guilty accepting all that money," she said. "Guilty and exploited at the same time, if you can understand that."

"I can understand that. I'd feel the same way. What did you do, turn him down?"

There was no doubt in her mind that that's what Graham would have done if it had been him; moral, upstanding, straight-arrow Graham. "No," she said miserably, "I told him I wanted a hundred and ten thousand dollars a year instead."

That took some explaining: how that was the amount that Kate had been getting, and Lee had asked for it to make a point, although she was a little unsure of what the point was; how she hadn't really expected Sawyer to consider it; how she hadn't *wanted* him to consider it, not really; how she wished he hadn't called her in the first place; how she wanted to *earn* any endorsement contract she ever got, not have it offered on a silver platter because she happened to be caught in the refracted limelight of a sensational murder.

"But you didn't tell him that," Graham said.

"No." She stared out the window. For a few seconds there were no sounds but the booming of the incoming surf and the long rattle of millions of pebbles as it slid out again. "I think the idea of that much money just paralyzed me. It's so seductive. It could mean so much to my golf game, to my sense of security. Well, there's nothing illegal about it, is there?" she said, abruptly irritated by his clear blue eyes, so carefully unjudgmental. "Well, is there?"

"No."

"Or unethical?"

No answer.

"It's done all the time, isn't it?" she said angrily. "That's the way they sell things. Nobody's asking me to lie, or to say I use equipment that I don't use, or—" She reached a hand around to rub the back of a neck that had begun to burn with a slow, deep ache. "Oh, hell," she said. "I just wouldn't feel right doing it. For me it'd be unethical; that's all there is to it. Besides," she added with a small smile, "Sawyer positively gives me the creeps, even long distance."

"So where does it stand now?"

She sighed. "Where it stands," she said, decisive all at once, "is that I'm going to tell him flat out I'm not interested, period." The moment she said it her spirits lifted.

He nodded, obviously pleased. "Anything else you can use my advice on? No other bothersome little moral dilemmas?"

"None," she said. Without realizing it she was still rubbing the back of her neck. Graham reached across, moved her hand out of the way, and slipped his own hand beneath her collar to knead her shoulders, his fingers warm and strong.

"How's that feel?"

"Mmm," she said, slowly rolling her head with her eyes closed. "Wonderful."

He leaned closer. With his other hand he brushed a few strands of hair from her forehead, softly stroked her cheek, and tipped her head gently toward his. He kissed her quietly, kindly, almost chastely. It was just the kind of kiss she needed. His mustache brushed her upper lip; it was softer than it looked, not bristly at all.

She let her fingers come up to touch the mustache, then, shyly, his jawline. "That was nice," she said. He smelled woodsy and clean, the way she'd expected him to.

"All right for starters," he said with a smile. "Nice to make your acquaintance, Miss Ofsted."

"Nice to make yours, Lieutenant."

"Hey, what are you doing for dinner Sunday night?"

"Having it with you," Lee answered, surprising herself, but pleasing herself too, and they both laughed again.

"Pick you up at Carmel Point after the tournament? Four o'clock, maybe?"

"Fine. . . . Er, no," she said, remembering her appointment with Farley. "I have to meet someone at four. How about five-thirty."

"Okay, five-thirty."

"Are we going to talk about police matters?"

"No." His clear eyes looked directly into hers. "Definitely no police matters."

He turned away and switched on the ignition. "I think we'd better get going. The captain doesn't take kindly to fooling around in unmarked police cars."

"Next time let's take a marked one," she said, and for the second time in a few hours they shared a small fit of silly, happy, irrepressible laughter.

12

AT THE LODGE, Lee was waved in through the open French doors of Peg's suite and greeted with a vigorous hug. "Hey, the day's results are in. You've advanced to sixteenth! Congratulations!"

"You're kidding!" It was better than she'd dared hope.

"Foster, Belski, and Yamura all blew it," Peg boomed. "And everybody on TV is talking about your birdie on the sixteenth. You're famous!"

Lee grinned. "I don't know how I had the nerve to try. How did our team do?"

"Twenty-second, how about that? I got three sleeves of Pro Staffs and twenty percent off a muffler job. I think you got a hundred and fifty dollars. Don't knock it."

"Who's knocking it?"

The telephone rang and Lee was motioned to a chair. "Fantastic," Peg said into the telephone after a moment. "Thanks a mill, Vi."

She hung up and bent to tug a pair of sandals onto her bare feet. "Forget the lesson; we have to hustle. That was one of my spies. Ben Tuckett just walked into the Giant Artichoke."

"Come again?"

"Kate's caddie, the mysterious Mr. Ben."

"That much I understood. But what did he walk into?"

"The Giant Artichoke. It's a roadside stand in Castroville. Fifteen, twenty miles from here." She cinched the belt of her Bermuda shorts a notch tighter around her chunky middle. "Let's go. We just might catch him."

"Wait a minute," Lee said. "I promised Graham I'd tell him if we heard where he was. I'd better call the police station."

Peg flopped histrionically back into the chair. "Are you serious? How long do you think the guy is going to stand there and wait?"

"No, I promised," Lee said, reaching for the telephone.

It was, Lee thought, the grandmotherly woman in the pantsuit who answered. Sorry, but Lieutenant Sheldon was not expected back until later in the afternoon. No, the car he was using did not have a working radio. Yes, he might call in, and in that case the message would be relayed. In the meantime, it would be given to Sergeant Rubio, assuming he could be found.

Peg was out of her chair before the receiver was back in place. "Okay, you kept your promise. Honor is preserved. Now let's *go*!"

Twenty minutes later she was pulling the BMW off Highway 1 and into the little town of Castroville. On the main street they passed under a big hanging banner ("Artichoke Capital of the World!") and turned into the parking lot of a sprawling structure that seemed to be a combination country store and restaurant. It really was named the Giant Artichoke, Lee saw, and the reason was apparent; at the entrance towered an impressively realistic artichoke made of green-painted reinforced concrete and standing well over fifteen feet high.

"They're big on artichokes around here," Peg explained in what might or might not have been a pun.

Inside the store, the giant-vegetable motif was repeated with subtle variations. The tomatoes were heaped in a red, tomato-shaped container five feet in diameter, the lemons in a mammoth, sunny lemon, the bananas in a colossal plastic banana. Eight or ten customers were browsing, but there was no sign of Mr. Ben. Lee and Peg went through the door into the restaurant section, and there they saw him, a wiry, teak-skinned black man of sixty, sitting alone at a table over a chocolate milkshake and a red-plaid cardboard container heaped with deep-fried chunks of something, apparently at peace with himself and the world.

"That's him," Lee said. "What do we do now?"

"Now," Peg said firmly, "we take the bull by the horns."

They walked up to him and Peg said, "Excuse me, but aren't you Ben Tuckett?"

He looked up from a French-fried morsel he had been about to pop into his mouth. "Yes, ma'am," he said.

"You were Kate O'Brian's caddie, weren't you?"

"Why, yes," he said. "Yes, I was." His voice was as soft as Peg's was hearty.

"You didn't leave an address with the caddie master. No one knew where to find you."

"Well, no," he said, as if this was a surprising new thought, "I don't suppose they would." He looked up at them politely.

Peg appeared to have run out of gas. "Hmm," she told him.

Lee joined in. "We're both in the Pacific-Western, Mr. Tuckett. This is Peg Fiske, and I'm Lee Ofsted."

"Yes, I know you, miss. You're a fine young golfer." He was still holding the morsel gracefully in his slender brown fingers, apparently refraining from eating out of courtesy. Hesitantly he half rose. "Would you ladies care to sit?"

"Thanks," Peg said as they sat down opposite him. "Go ahead and eat, Mr. Tuckett. What's that you're having? It smells marvelous." Peg was not hard to distract, given the right stimulus.

"It surely does," Tuckett said with his first visible show of enthusiasm. "They're fried artichokes. I always get some when I'm in the area. They cut the artichoke hearts in quarters, you see, and marinate them, but the secret is the seasoned batter. They won't tell you what's in it, but they'll sell you a bag. If you ask me—"

Peg had recovered her impetus and again took the bull by the horns. "Excuse me, Mr. Tuckett. We're aware that Kate let you go not long before she was killed. We'd like very much to know why."

His gentle eyes widened. "Let me go?"

"Fired you," Peg explained tersely.

"No, ma'am, excuse me, but that's just not so," Mr. Ben said with dignity. "I resigned from caddying." He permitted himself a gentle smile. "Or as I prefer to say, I retired." He placed the artichoke piece in his mouth at last and fastidiously wiped his fingers one by one on a paper napkin.

They both stared at him. No one really knew what happened to old caddies, but they didn't retire. Not without pension plans, or medical insurance, or vision-care benefits, or the rest of it. They simply melted away, perhaps into other more stable pursuits. One day someone would ask, "Say, whatever happened to old Scooter? Haven't seen him around for a while." Others would agree or shake their heads absently, and that would be the end of old Scooter, except in blessed memory.

Mr. Ben, who seemed to note their surprise, explained with quiet pride: For fourteen years he had worked for Kate almost exclusively. In that time fortune had been good to her, and she had been good to him. As a single man with simple tastes, he had managed to invest much of his income, and now the time had come for him to settle down. That was all there was to it.

"I have an interest in three condominium complexes not far from Atlanta, you see, with a cozy little bachelor apartment for myself in one of them. With the income from my money market account and CDs, I can live very comfortably."

Lee exchanged a quick glance with Peg. Money market account? CDs? Condominiums? Is *this* what happened to old Scooter and the rest of them? She doubted it. Mr. Ben, she suspected, was one of a kind.

"Let me ask this," Peg said. "What happened to make you retire so suddenly?"

"Suddenly?"

"Well, you must have caught Kate by surprise because she didn't have a chance to line up a permanent caddie for her practice round on Wednesday. And later on she was shagging her own balls on the practice range.''

This seemed to disturb him. ''Shagging her own balls? I'm very sorry to hear that.'' He shook his head and consoled himself with another piece of artichoke. ''But I have to say—with respect—it was her own doing.''

Early in the season, Mr. Ben went on, Kate had told him that she herself planned to retire after the WPGL Open in August, and he had replied that he might as well just up and retire alongside her. But then, since she didn't do well in the Open, she decided to stay with it for one more tournament in the hope that she could quit with flair, and although he had already made other plans, he naturally agreed to caddy for her. So it went for two more tournaments, and when it came time for the Pacific-Western, she told him positively that she wouldn't play. But by the time Mr. Ben had gotten back to his cozy little bachelor apartment near Atlanta, there was a telephone message awaiting him: Kate would play after all, and could he possibly come? She wouldn't feel right with anybody but him.

''Well, that was only natural,'' Mr. Ben allowed, ''so I packed up and came right out here. But then she changed her mind again, and said she *wouldn't* play . . .'' He slid the emptied carton away from him with a sigh. ''I just had to tell her that I had other responsibilities now, and wouldn't be able to come at her beck and call any more.''

''You fought over it?'' Peg said.

''Well, now, I wouldn't say we fought. No, I wouldn't say that. I suppose we did have words.''

''When was this?''

''Wednesday morning.'' Peg's aggressive questioning was beginning to make him edgy. He moved uneasily in his chair and his soft eyes darted from one of them to the other.

''But Kate shot a practice round later that day, and she was on the practice tee after that,'' Peg said. ''And she was listed on the roster when she was killed. So she must have changed her mind one more time and decided to play after all.''

''So it would seem,'' Mr. Ben said cautiously.

"Mr. Tuckett, you and Kate split up on Wednesday, but today's Saturday and you're still here. Why is that?"

Mr. Ben drew himself up. "Mrs. O'Brian's memorial service is tomorrow," he said simply. "How could I leave before then?" He cleared his throat. "No offense intended, but perhaps if you ladies would be kind enough to tell me in what way you're concerned in this . . . ?"

"Benjamin Gibson Tuckett?" a voice behind Lee boomed.

She turned to see a burly, uniformed police officer. Beside him was Sergeant Rubio.

"Why, yes," Mr. Ben said to them.

"I wonder if we could talk to you, sir," the officer said.

"Well . . . yes, of course."

"It might be better if we did it at our office, sir. We'll be glad to drive you there and back."

Mr. Ben glanced nervously at Lee, then at the policeman. His Adam's apple bobbed. "Am I . . . am I under arrest?" He held his hands out in front of him as if he expected to be handcuffed.

"No, sir, not at all," Rubio said. "We just have a few questions we hope you can help us with. It shouldn't take long."

Mr. Ben rose soberly. He might have been on his way to the gas chamber.

"Would it be all right," he asked meekly, "if I . . . if I stopped at the counter and bought a bag of seasoned batter?"

"How about some French-fried artichokes?" Peg said to Lee after Mr. Ben made his modest purchase and left with the police. "I'm buying."

"No, thanks. I just had lunch a little while ago."

"Well, so did I. What's that got to do with anything? I'm talking about a snack."

Lee had a cup of lemonade instead and they talked over their session with Mr. Ben while Peg spiritedly and methodically demolished her artichokes.

"Did you know," she asked between mouthfuls, "that Kate had done all that waffling about playing in the tournament?"

"No."

"Me neither. I didn't know they'd let you get away with that. I thought once you told the officials you were out, you were out."

"Once *I* told them I was out I'd be out. But if you were Kate they'd be inclined to give you a little more leeway. Kind of the way they'd be if Martina Navratilova did a little waffling about playing at your local racquet club." Thoughtfully she sucked a pillar of lemonade up with her straw. "I wonder if it's important."

"Important how?"

"Well, think about how Nick Pittman might feel about it, for example. Here he is directing his first tournament, telling everyone the great Kate O'Brian will be there, and then she pulls out."

"But the last anybody heard she was back in."

"Was she? Maybe she changed her mind again out there on the practice tee and he finally exploded out of frustration. Or maybe he figured murdering her right there at Carmel Point would be the best publicity the tournament could get."

"Which it was," Peg said. "Attendance is almost twenty percent over the estimates." She used her finger to mop up a few remaining crisps of batter. "I don't know, though. Are you really serious?"

Lee shrugged. "I'm not sure. *Somebody* killed Kate for *some* reason." She bent her straw in two and shoved her emptied cup aside. "What do you think about Mr. Ben?"

"If that man is a murderer," Peg said, "I'm Godzilla."

13

GOLF MAY BE the clumsiest of spectator sports. Going to a golf tournament is like going to a baseball game and finding out that most of it is being played in other stadiums from which incomplete and ambiguous reports issue from time to time. No one has ever seen a complete golf tournament, even with the help of television. No one can be sure of exactly what's going on until it's over. While you are cheering your favorite as he expertly drops in his final putt on the eighteenth, he may actually be falling a stroke behind as someone else sinks one half a mile away on the tenth.

To make it more comprehensible, major tournaments set up leaderboards at various places around the course. With the help of an army of people with two-way radios, these big scoreboards continuously monitor the progress of the ten players with the lowest scores of the moment. Fans find this helpful, but golfers are divided. Some like to know exactly how they're doing; others hate the pressure, preferring to play their own games and not their competitors'.

Before Sunday's pro's-only final round Lee had never given much thought to which camp she was in. It was not a problem you had to worry about if you didn't spend much time in the top ten. From eleventh down, you just played your best and hoped your hardest, and when it was over you and everybody else would find out how you did.

On Carmel Point's par-4, 400-yard fourteenth hole, however, Lee concluded that leaderboards were definitely something she could do without. She was in a threesome with Wilma Snell and a lanky, quiet Georgian named Patti Bea Sweetwater. Lee and Patti had started the day tied for sixteenth at 221, five strokes over par for the first three rounds. Wilma had been two strokes behind. Over the first thirteen holes Lee had had another strong day, and with a birdie on the eleventh she had moved three strokes ahead of Patti. Wilma was doing well too, but Lee had so far managed to remain a stroke or two ahead of her. Beyond that, of course, she had no idea of how she was doing relative to the rest of the field.

Until she happened to glance up as she took a practice swing with her pitching wedge on the approach to the fourteenth green. A course marshal had just pulled the name *Owens* out of the tenth-place slot on the big green leaderboard, and now he was inserting *Ofsted*—My God, right up there with *Alcott*, and *Bradley*, and *Okamoto*! She watched avidly as he put up her scores.

"Come on, Lee, let's go," Lou prompted.

"Lou, look." Dumbstruck, she pointed at the board with her club.

"Yeah, big deal," he said gruffly. "We still got five holes to go. Just play your game. Forget about the board."

Forget about the board? How could she forget about the board? In a field of seventy-two she was *tenth*. . . . No, not tenth, but tied for *ninth*, only seven strokes behind the leader with just six holes to go. *Ninth!* She'd never done anywhere near so well this late in a major tournament.

Lou clasped her arm, something he hadn't ever done before. "Lee," he said, peering worriedly up at her, "don't freeze up on me. We're doing great."

"Right, Lou," she said absently, still staring at the board.

It was going to take careful play from here on. No more reckless chances. Don't even think about moving up. Play it safe, hold on. Go for the pars. Ninth place—What would that be? Eight thousand dollars? Nine thousand? It was almost as much as she'd made all year in twenty-three tournaments.

She lined up carefully, feet close together, weight a little forward, stance open, trying to smooth her shallow breathing. It should have been an easy forty-yard loft to the green over a kidney-shaped bunker, but her swing was constrained and jerky. She topped the ball, rocketing a line drive only inches off the grass, directly into the one place she wanted to avoid. To an accompanying groan from the gallery, the ball plopped into the sand trap, and not only the sand trap but the forward wall of the sand trap, imbedding itself below an overhanging lip that made it impossible to shoot toward the green on the next stroke. So much for glory, she thought. And so much for par on the fourteenth. She'd be grateful to get out of this one with a bogey.

Graham was twenty minutes into his jog, rounding the rocky, surf-battered outcropping of Point Pinos, when he finally realized what was bothering him, and he spun immediately to head back toward his apartment. It was a line in Rubio's report; Rubio's deadeningly thorough eighteen-page report on Kate O'Brian's business affairs.

He increased his pace back down Sunset Drive and took a shortcut across the cypress groves and iceplant-dotted dunes of the Asilomar Conference Center. From the main gate it was three blocks to his apartment off Sinex Avenue.

When he got there the television set was still on. Earlier he had been going cursorily through the report and watching the Pacific-Western on and off, hoping to catch a glimpse of Lee, but the closest he'd come was when they'd shown her name with a +5 after it as part of a long, long list. The mind-numbing combination of Rubio's prose and the golf match (he had tried to approach it with an open mind, but it was *slow*) had driven him out for a run. And it had worked. Something had clicked.

He showered quickly and turned down the volume of the set just as *Ofsted* rolled up the screen again, this time with a +3. He hoped that was an improvement. The report was still on the table he'd built into the bay window overlooking the park, and he sat down to it with a mug of coffee from the pot that had been on the range since 9 A.M.

It was on page two of Rubio's meticulously formatted statistical appendix; section 1.21 (Current Income, Business, Salaried). He put his finger on the line.

Annual Retaining Fee, Sawyer.................... $140,000

His interview notes were in his office desk five miles away, but he remembered well enough what Stratton had told him about Kate's annual retainer from Sawyer, and it wasn't $140,000. According to Stratton, it was $110,000. And Lee had said the same thing: $110,000. She had heard it from Kate herself.

Rubio's information was accurate, of course. He had called Sawyer Sports Equipment in Baltimore and talked to the comptroller and to Ellis Sawyer himself. This Graham knew because the sergeant had submitted a scrupulously detailed expense form for his signature ten minutes after hanging up.

Graham lifted the mug thoughtfully to his lips. Was he on to something, or could Stratton have made an honest mistake? No, he thought, he was on to something, all right. During the interview the manager had been cagey and vague about the amount; Graham had had to press him. Now he thought he understood why: Sawyer *was* paying Kate $140,000; that was true enough. But Kate was getting only $110,000; that was true too. The catch was that there was a middleman. And the middleman was Farley Stratton.

It wouldn't have had to be a very complicated scam. All Stratton would have had to do was to negotiate a $140,000 contract with Sawyer in Kate's name, then go back and tell Kate it was for $110,000. There would have been the necessity to forge her signature on the contract that went to Sawyer and Ellis Sawyer's signature on the copy that went to Kate, but why would that be a problem? They were hardly likely to scrutinize the signatures.

Once that was done, it would have been virtually untraceable unless someone got suspicious and poked around. The Sawyer checks, after all, would not have been made out to Kate but to Farley; that was the way it worked. Then, from his own checking account, Farley would have written a check to Kate—minus the odd $30,000 a year, which could be laundered a hundred different ways.

How hard could it have been to bring off? Not very. As long as Kate and the company were kept out of touch—except through him—Stratton was safe. And that wouldn't have been too difficult, what with Kate living on the West Coast and Sawyer Sports Equipment being located in Baltimore, where there were no WPGL stops. And Ellis Sawyer himself was known as a near-recluse who had little to do with his sports stars once they were signed up.

The only thing Stratton would have had to worry about was the possibility that Kate might talk about her contract, perhaps even with a reporter, and word might get back to Sawyer. But even there, Stratton had covered himself. Hadn't Lee told him that Kate was forbidden by her contract to discuss its terms? That her mention of them to Lee during a drive had been a slip?

Stratton was more clever than Graham had given him credit for being. He might or might not be a murderer (Had Kate found out? Quarreled with him? Threatened to expose him?), but he was certainly a crook. The question was: What to do now? There wasn't enough to justify an arrest yet, but Stratton was scheduled to fly back to Los Angeles the next afternoon, and Graham didn't like—

The telephone rang in the kitchen. Graham remained in his chair, letting the answering machine handle it but listening to the loudspeaker.

"This is Tessa at the office," the voice intoned in the machinelike way that people address machines. "I just got a call from a Mrs. Kollar at Naturalgrown Chicken Farms near Salinas. She has some information about some chicken blood, if I understood her right, and she was told to talk to you, so I told her I'd try to get hold of you. Her number—"

By that time he was at the kitchen counter cutting in. He jotted down the number and dialed it at once.

"Mrs. Kollar? This is Lieutenant Sheldon."

"Oh, Lieutenant, I'm sorry to bother you on a Sunday. The girl said you weren't working today."

"That's all right, Mrs. Kollar. I appreciate your calling."

"It's about this chicken blood. The policeman who was here Friday talked to Leon—that's my husband, Leon Kollar. I was in San Jose, and Leon, he forgot about it until just now. But I was the one who gave the man the blood."

Graham had a familiar and welcome sensation—the feeling of a net drawing in on itself. "What man was that, Mrs. Kollar?"

"Well, he bought a chicken, and he asked for some blood to go with it because he wanted to use it in a stuffing. I remember, because I didn't hear of anybody doing this since the old country. I asked him did he want blood from the same chicken, because that's the way we did it in olden times, but he said it didn't matter. But I gave it to him anyway. All the same, it struck me as a funny thing."

"Did you get his name, Mrs. Kollar?"

"No, why would I get his name? But I remember what he looked like. You want a description?"

"Very much."

"A big man, not a shrimp, with a lot of fat on his bones. Also a wonderful tan, like a movie star. And dressed sharp, not like a bum." Graham heard paper rustle. She had made notes before calling. "A wealthy man too; you know how I knew? He had a mouthful of gold like Fort Knox."

"Thank you, Mrs. Kollar. Could you identify him if you saw him again?"

"Sure I could. In a second. What did he do anyway?"

When Graham hung up he slapped the countertop with satisfaction. It was Farley Stratton, all right, and it was time to haul in that net. First, of course, they would have to find him. He called Tessa and asked her to have Captain Bushell and Sergeant Rubio meet him at the office.

"On Sunday? The captain's not going to be too happy about it," Tessa said.

"He'll be happy," Graham said.

14

LEE DIDN'T MANAGE even a bogey on the fourteenth; she wound up with a humiliating double bogey, and her name was gone from the leaderboard before she got to the fifteenth tee.

"What the hell," Lou said. "So we choked up a little."

"Just a little," Lee said with a small smile. Lou was being generous. That miserable shot into the bunker had cost him a good hundred dollars. She didn't want to think about what it had cost her.

"Hey, don't worry about it," he went on unselfishly. "It's only natural. You'll get used to seeing your name up on the board."

Maybe, but not that day. Lee holed out on the eighteenth entirely unaware of her position. As a result of this relatively blissful ignorance she had relaxed and managed to score two birdies and two pars on the last four holes. Not enough to regain the leaderboard, but very good indeed.

After she signed out there was time to run over and look at the big cumulative scoreboard. They were just posting her scores, and at two over par she was now all alone in eleventh place, with no one likely to displace her. Her brief glimpse of glory at the fourteenth hole had come and gone, and now eleventh place was very sweet, a marvelous way to end the year. She found a copy of the WPGL Player Guide on a folding table and pretended to browse casually in it, but turned eagerly to the purse breakdown chart, holding her breath while she scanned the columns. Eleventh place in a $400,000 tournament would bring . . .

Seven thousand six hundred dollars. She sank onto a folding chair, shaky with happiness. Added to what she'd earned before, her winnings for the year would come to $17,000, enough to place no worse than hundredth on the money list. She was *in* for next year. Not exempt, but in. No tense, grueling return to the Qualifying School in October, and no extension on Cobe's loan. And no longer any reason for even a glimmer of apprehension over turning down Ellis Sawyer's mind-boggling offer.

Well, maybe a glimmer.

There was a message from Peg in the clubhouse. "Fantastic round! Super! Congratulations! Call."

She was equally exuberant on the telephone. "You were great! Sara and Linda and I watched the whole round on 'Wide World of Sports' at the Highlands Inn, munching popcorn and rooting for you."

I made $7,600! Lee wanted to shout.

"When they showed you on television," Peg said, "Linda practically had a fit."

"They showed me on television? Really?"

Peg's voice became a little more subdued. "Uh, yes. That's the good news."

"What's the bad news?"

"Well, they only showed you hitting one ball."

Lee groaned. "The one on the fourteenth, right after I made the leaderboard. The line drive into the sand trap."

" 'Fraid so. But look at the bright side."

"What's the bright side?"

"Well, now they have a new shot they can use for the agony-of-defeat bit. Maybe they'll give you residuals."

Lee laughed. "Oh, thanks. That's bright, all right."

"Lee, are you free for breakfast tomorrow morning? I've been doing some more thinking about Kate, and I think we ought to talk. And I want to hear how your session with Farley goes."

"Good. What time?"

"I'll pick you up at eight— Oops."

"Oops, what?"

"Aren't you seeing Graham tonight?"

"That's right, but I'm free tomorrow morning."

"Yes, well, I was just thinking—You might be, er, still occupied at breakfast time. Maybe we better make it lunch."

"Peg, I'm having dinner with him, I'm not going to bed with him. I just met him a few days ago."

"I know, but things are different now than when I was on the loose. You kids today—"

"Peg," Lee said with some asperity, "I hate to tell you this, but you are one sexual revolution behind. In any case, I am not spending the night with Graham. I will see you for breakfast at eight A.M. tomorrow, all right?"

Peg sent a growly laugh over the telephone. "Okay," she grumbled, "but I don't see the point of these new sexual mores if you're just going to waste them when opportunity knocks."

Lee was laughing as she hung up, but she stopped when she glanced at her watch. Three-fifty. She barely had time to make her meeting with Farley Stratton.

15

GRAHAM WAS WRONG. Captain Bushell was not at all happy. "It's not enough," he said testily. "What do we arrest him for, suspicion of defacing a golf club?"

"Don't forget that tricky business with the Sawyer contract."

"And whose jurisdiction is that? What's it got to do with Carmel PD, for Christ's sake?"

"Yes, there is the question of false arrest," Rubio concurred gravely.

"Look," Bushell said, "all we know for sure—assuming we get a positive ID out of it—is that the guy bought a chicken and asked for some blood to go along with it. Everything else is—hell, all it is, is—"

"Surmise?" said Rubio.

"Yeah," Bushell said. "Surmise." He jabbed a finger at Graham. "Let me ask you this," he said, and jiggled in his chair the way he did when he thought he was about to deliver a crusher. "Let me ask you this. Why would this guy first stick the murder weapon in Ofsted's bag so it looked like she did it, and then a couple days later pull this cockamamie stunt that's got to prove she *didn't* do it?" He jerked his head belligerently, driving the point in with his chin.

It wasn't a crusher but it was a question Graham had no answer for. "All right," he said, "I admit there are still a lot of questions, but all we've got is another twenty-four hours. The guy leaves for L.A. tomorrow. The least we can do is put him under surveillance while—''

"Surveillance!'' Bushell interrupted with a laugh. "You think you're still in Oakland or something? Who am I supposed to use for surveillance, the reserves?''

Graham was prevented from answering by a buzz from Bushell's telephone. The captain picked it up, listened stolidly for a few seconds, asked a few succinct and policeman-like questions ("Where?'' "When?''), and hung up. When he looked at Graham and Rubio his expression was different.

"Farley Stratton's dead. A couple of birdwatchers found his body.''

"Where?'' Rubio asked. "When?''

"Near Fort Ord, on the beach. At one-thirty. With two twenty-five-caliber slugs in his head.''

Rubio frowned. "Twenty-five caliber?''

"That's right,'' Bushell said with a nod. "One of those little-bitty women's guns. A Beretta Jetfire, something like that.''

Graham, who had been standing, sank slowly into Bushell's single side chair and looked dreamily through the high window at the sky.

"Dead,'' he murmured, almost to himself. "Then who . . .''

Wilma Snell's blocky, solid form loomed abruptly over Lee. "Do you want to go a few holes, Lee?''

Lee looked up with a start. While waiting for Farley she had been at a table in the Cormorant, happily absorbed with a pocket calculator and a notepad, computing the many ways $7,600 was going to make life easier. Now she glanced at her watch. It was 4:25. Apparently she had been stood up by Farley Stratton. The crud, to quote Peg.

"Come on,'' Wilma said. "It's practically deserted. We'll have it all to ourselves.''

The fact that Wilma should want to get back out on the course at the end of a grueling four-day tournament was not in itself surprising. Professional golfers spend a lot more time on the practice tee and in practice rounds than weekend golfers do. And they are more likely to keep swinging away after a day in the 60s or low 70s than one in the 80s, in the ever-renewing hope that they can permanently engrave on their minds and muscles whatever mysterious and elusive thing it was they were doing so well.

What *was* surprising was that Wilma should ask her along. There was no hostility between the two of them, but no rapport either; Lee had always felt a faint, formless unease in the older golfer's presence, like what an unwelcome child foisted on a crabby, chapfallen aunt might feel. During the day's round they had not exchanged half a dozen sentences.

"I don't know . . ." she said hesitantly. "I'm meeting someone at six o'clock."

"Time enough for five or six holes," Wilma pressed.

Lee looked at her watch again. An hour and a half until Graham came to pick her up. That was a long time to sit and wait in the Cormorant, even with $7,600 to plan for. "Okay," she said, reaching for her bag, "you're on."

In the golden late afternoon, after the bustle of the tournament, Carmel Point was at its best, green and mellow, and rimmed by a burnished sea. A few golfers, alone or in pairs, moved indolently along velvet fairways trailed by long shadows. Only a clattering, low-flying helicopter spoiled the otherworldly calm.

Wilma and Lee skipped the first few long but unchallenging holes and picked up the course at the rolling fourth, where it doubled back past the Cormorant. It was hard to understand why Wilma had wanted company; she was no less tight-lipped and morose than usual. On their third hole, after Wilma had led off with a soft, perfectly placed two-iron to the right corner of a narrow, left-leaning dogleg, Lee tried to liven things up.

"What a lovely shot!" she exclaimed as she got out her own two-iron. "I wish I could place them like that."

Wilma's response was a mutter and a shrug as she bent to pull up the tee she'd placed flush with the turf.

"That was a wonderful round you played today," Lee persisted. "It was just luck you didn't catch me." Wilma had ended up only one behind her, tied for twelfth with three others. "And to think, you almost didn't get to play at all."

Wilma looked up aggressively. "What's that supposed to mean?"

Lee began to regret leaving her calculator and her solitary table. "Well, only that you did so well, and they wouldn't even have let you play if not for—for what happened to Kate."

"The bitch," Wilma said distinctly.

Lee stiffened. "What?"

Wilma rounded on her. "What's the matter, am I not supposed to say it because she's dead? Did she give a damn about *me*? 'Yes, I'll play; no, I won't play; yes, I'll play; no, I won't play.' " She had twisted up her face and mewled the words in a horrible way that sounded nothing like Kate, nothing like anything human.

"Wilma—"

Lee began to back away, a terrible understanding beginning to ease its way into her insides like an icy blade. Why hadn't she thought of it before? Why hadn't any of them thought of it? Mr. Ben had told them how Kate had dithered about playing in the tournament, had changed her mind time after time. To Kate it was nothing one way or the other. But to Wilma . . . to tired, aging, slipping Wilma, who had missed the cut by one in the qualifying round, it was everything. With Kate out of it, with Kate dead, Wilma was back in the tournament with a final opportunity to battle back into the exempt class for next year, a final chance to avoid the debilitating grunginess of Monday qualifiers, of being a has-been among the rabbits.

Two pink blotches had leaped out on her thick neck, two livid, bruised-looking spots on her cheeks. "It was a big joke to her. What did she care about how I felt?" She advanced on Lee, gripping the heavy two-iron. "What do *you* know about what it feels like—"

Lee threw up her arm. "Wilma, don't . . . !"

Wilma stopped, blinking as if someone had doused her with a bucket of cold water.

"Don't what?"

At precisely that moment there was a crunch behind them,

on the gravel path leading from the previous green. Miraculously, Milt Sawyer appeared, fat and beaming.

"Well, hi there," he said cheerily. "You two were just great today."

Lee sagged with relief. "Milt!" The word seemed to rush out of her. She realized that she'd been holding her breath.

"Want me to play on through?" he asked. He was carrying a light nylon bag of clubs.

"No!" she squeaked, then sucked in a breath and steadied herself. "No, why don't you join us, Milt? We'd love to have you."

He swelled and simpered. "Well, all right, I suppose I could do that."

Wilma's color had settled back to its usual lusterless dun. She seemed to have shrunken, as if a spotlight that had been on her had been turned off. "No," she said expressionlessly. "I've had enough. I don't want to play any more." She glanced at the iron in her hand as if she were surprised to find it there, then sheathed it in her bag. With a last, sullen, unreadable look at Lee (A threat? An entreaty?) she slouched heavily away toward the clubhouse, moving in and out of the black, needle-pointed shadows of the pine trees that fringed the fairway.

Milt watched her go. "Did I interrupt something?" he asked. Then he took a closer look at Lee. "You look *awful*. What's the matter?"

She shook her head. She could feel her heartbeat, shallow and unsteady. "I'm not sure. Thank goodness you came along. It was awful. I don't know if I was imagining it, or . . ."

"What?" Milt peeped with an alarmed expression. "What, what?"

"Look, could I just sit down a minute and catch my breath?"

"Of course, sure. Can I get you something? Would you rather be alone?"

"No!" she said quickly. "Don't go, please. Let's go down to the beach." She pointed at a break in the bushes about five yards from the tee box, where a stairway of wooden railroad ties was cut into the steep side of the bluff, zigzagging twenty feet down to a rocky little inlet.

"I've played this course half a dozen times and I never knew this was here," Milt said as they worked their way down. "Walked right by these steps last week and never saw them. Of course I had a Nassau game going with Hale and Gerry, so you can imagine I had to watch them pretty carefully." He shook his head, laughing. "That Gerry."

Lee sank down onto a rock formation scooped out by wind and water into a concave basin, like a beanbag chair. The stored heat in the stone felt good against the small of her back. Offshore, on a jumble of rocks beyond the surf a colony of sea lions sprawled in the fading sunlight, flopping and quarreling.

She turned her face toward the sun and closed her eyes, leaning her cheek on the cool, familiar shaft of the two-iron, making herself breathe slowly in and out. The primitive, fishy reek of the sea lions on the breeze was somehow reassuring. Her pulse began to slow down.

"Gerry who?" she asked.

"Ford," Milt said as if it should have been obvious.

Lee smiled with her eyes still closed. The world was returning to normal.

"You don't know if you imagined what?" Milt said after a moment.

"I thought . . . for a minute I thought Wilma was . . ."

Wilma was what? Going to kill her? Going to confess to murdering Kate? Already it was receding, telescoping, becoming ambiguous and unreal. Had Wilma really been threatening her with the club, or had Lee's imagination gotten the better of her?

"What did you imagine, Lee?" Milt asked again from behind her.

She began to answer, then stopped in midsentence, first puzzled then frightened by the queer, stifled quality of his voice. Instinctively she stood up and turned to face him, the hair on the back of her neck prickling like a wary dog's.

It was that involuntary, reflexive action that saved her life. As she spun around she heard a snap like a stick breaking, hardly audible above the surf. Her left forearm stung suddenly, as if she'd rubbed against a nettle. Later she would be amazed at her dim-wittedness, but for a full second she was utterly stupefied, not understanding. She fancied at first that he had slapped her arm, but he was too far away; four or five feet. Had he hit her with something? Thrown a stick at her?

Her arm continued to burn. Confused, she looked down at it. There was a narrow, long depression just below the elbow, not deep but peculiar: a gray-white furrow. Gingerly, with the fingers of her other hand she touched it. The skin was greasy and hot, and flecked with bits of what looked like black pepper. A few droplets of blood were beginning to seep through the skin at one end. She stared, hardly able to believe it. A bullet graze?

Was it Milt, then, and not Wilma at all? Had it been Milt all along? Dumbfounded, she lifted her eyes to him. He stared back at her, his mouth working silently.

"Did you—did you just *shoot* me?" she said, and a tight, hysterical little giggle almost broke from her throat at the absurdity of the question.

Milt didn't answer. The only sounds were the hiss of the surf and the grumbling yawps of the sea lions. In his right hand was a small, silvery pistol that looked like something you'd buy for $2.99 at the checkout counter in Safeway; or maybe something that would sprout a cigarette lighter when you pulled the trigger. He was holding it at belt height, and now he raised it slowly to point at her face, not the way her army instructor had demonstrated, with arm extended and wrist cradled by the other hand, but in a cramped, old-womanish kind of way, with his round, bearish shoulders hunched and the gleaming, harmless-looking little gun in front of his chin. He was panting, blowing out his cheeks like a man underwater.

Dazedly, she remembered that she was still holding her two-iron, and she knew that if she had any chance at all, she had to act now. She tensed her muscles, bobbed to the side, and jabbed at the hand that held the gun.

But she moved in a sort of sickly dream, weak-jointed and nauseated, not believing that this could really be happening, yet at the same time certain that she was about to die. Her jab with the iron was tentative and feeble, and Milt was able to grab the club head with his free hand. He pulled with unsuspected strength, almost jerking it away from her, but she caught it with both hands and hung on fiercely, twisting and pulling, surprised to hear herself sobbing.

Milt tried to club her with the gun, but she managed to curl her head away from him, taking a numbing sidewise blow on the corner of her mouth from the heel of his hand. She tightened her grasp and dug in more firmly, afraid to let go of the club, and Milt struggled against her, red-faced and staring, matching her sobs with strained, rising little bleats.

Why, he's more terrified than I am, she realized with dull surprise, and the thought was calming, stabilizing. Her mind suddenly cleared; the world came back into focus. It was only Milt Sawyer, for God's sake. Who said she was doomed?

As she'd learned in her brief few days of army combat training she relaxed abruptly, letting go of the club just as he tugged viciously. Milt stumbled backward with it for a few steps and fell heavily on his back with a *whoosh* that must have emptied his lungs. The club went one way, the gun the other, skittering over the sand. Lee was on it almost before it stopped, then jumped back, pointing it at him from a crouch.

"Don't move!" she said, her voice seeming to come from a long way off. Her heart was thudding more rapidly than ever. What was she supposed to do if he *did* move? Shoot him?

He moved. He got slowly to his thick knees, watching her all the time.

"I'm warning you," she said, waving the gun at him and backing up a step. Damn, that was a mistake. She should have held her ground. "I mean it, Milt." She didn't like the sound of her voice, scratchy and unstrung.

"You won't shoot me," he said breathily, getting to his feet and taking a single, testing step toward her. "Put the gun down, Lee. I won't hurt you, I promise."

She checked the safety and clicked back the breech just to show him she knew the way a semiautomatic worked. He paused, momentarily irresolute, then took another measured step, never taking his eyes off her.

She willed herself to stand her ground but her skitterish legs wouldn't obey; she backed away again, cursing herself. "Stay where you are, Milt," she said, putting as much threat as she could into it.

"You won't shoot me, Lee," he said again, half cocky, half pleading. Another step. A wan, hideous smile. "This is just a misunderstanding, isn't it?"

"Milt, I mean it. I'll shoot."

But would she? Why hadn't she done it already? Twice she had warned him not to move, twice he had come toward her, and both times it was she who had given way. Her hand was trembling so violently she was afraid she might drop the gun, but she did her best to level it at the center of his chest.

He came a step closer. She could smell his sweat; his shirt was soaked with it.

"One more step, Milt," she said. "I'll do it; I'm warning you." Her scalp itched ferociously but she didn't dare move. She prayed that he was bluffing, that he would see she meant it and stop.

For she would shoot him; she knew that now. He was only six feet from her, and she was up against the base of the rocky shelf that formed the cove, with no room to run any more. And she wouldn't stand there meekly and be killed. But he was a heavy man; she doubted that a single shot from this puny weapon would stop him. What if she fired and he kept coming? Would she have to shoot him again, and yet again? Would he manage to reach her, bloody and groaning, like some nightmare horror, groping with fat hands for her throat while she pumped bullet after bullet into his body?

Slowly Milt took the step she had forbidden him, the smile on his face now calcified into a dreadful rictus.

Lee squeezed back against the smooth, rocky wall. "My God, my God," she whispered frantically. How could this be happening? Grimacing, trying to watch him but to unfocus her eyes to avoid seeing what must happen, she tensed her finger on the trigger. There would be no more words. One more step and . . .

"Freeze!"

Graham's voice? For a moment she thought it was a dream, a timely hallucination ordered up by her frightened psyche: Lieutenant Sheldon, come to the rescue in the nick of time. But it was real, thank God. Milt looked as startled as she was. They both stood, rigid and frozen, only a few feet apart. In the distance, the incurious seals went on gripping at each other.

"Back away from her," Graham ordered, his voice thinned by the breeze but brimming with menace and authority. "Slowly. Keep your hands away from your body."

Milt, who had never stopped staring at Lee, finally lowered his eyes and began to back away, his shoulders tensed, as if he expected a bullet in the back of the neck. The way Graham sounded, Lee didn't blame him.

Now she finally dared to look up at where the voice was coming from. There on the bluff, at the top of the steps, was Graham, with Rubio at his side. Graham was on one knee, in a shooting posture that would have won approval from her old army instructor: right arm stiffly extended, steadied at the wrist by a firm left hand, body as taut and balanced as a panther's. And the revolver in his hand was no toy but an ugly, honest-to-goodness gun, black and stubby, with a squat, flaring barrel. Rubio, with a similar weapon, looked a little less dangerous, but more than intimidating enough. Both men's guns were fixed unwaveringly on Milt, moving as he moved.

With the flood of relief that drenched her, Lee's bones seemed to turn to wax. The little handgun was suddenly too heavy to hold up; her fingers had no feeling. She let her arm drop to her side. The pistol clacked against the rock and fell to the sand.

Graham muttered a few words to Rubio and shoved his revolver down into a shoulder holster inside his windbreaker. Did he always wear a gun? What an odd thought.

While Rubio followed very slowly, keeping his gun on Milt, Graham ran down the steps. Lee thought he was going to collar Milt, but he left him to Rubio, coming to her instead.

"Are you all right?"

"Yes, of course I am. But thank heavens you—"

She stopped. He was peering at her face, slowly raising his hand to touch the side of her mouth. To her surprise his fingers came away with blood on them. She'd forgotten Milt had cuffed her.

"Lee—" he began, his eyes cloudy with worry.

"No, really," she said. "I'm fine." Suddenly afraid she was going to burst into tears, she forced herself to smile brightly. She almost batted her eyelashes. "He sort of hit me by accident," she said inanely. "He didn't really mean to hurt me."

He grasped her upper arm gently, turning up the bullet crease. "Did he shoot at you by accident too?" he said gruffly. But his touch was tender. She could barely feel his fingertips as they traced the outline of the groove. He looked as if he were in pain himself.

Whatever it was that had been holding her together finally gave way. She began to shake, not just her hands but the muscles of her thighs and back. Her teeth chattered.

"Graham," she managed to quaver, "I know you're on duty and everything, but I need to be hugged something awful."

His arms were around her so fast she didn't have a chance to lift her hands from her sides. She was folded into him, wrapped in the woodsy, male smell of him, drawing strength from his strength, her forehead against the smooth, comforting fabric of his windbreaker. After a few long, steadying seconds she felt her heartbeat slow, and she lifted her hands to clasp him lightly around the waist.

"Thank you," she said. "I'm all right now. I don't know what was the matter with me. I don't cry very often."

"Poststress reaction," he said. "Too much adrenaline too fast. It happens to me too after something like this."

She smiled. "I'll bet."

He smiled back. "Sure. I have to get a big hug from the captain." Gently he set her away from him, still holding her arms. "Sure you're okay?"

She nodded. "Yes."

"Got any cuffs?" said Sergeant Rubio.

Graham looked over his shoulder. "What?"

Rubio gestured toward Milt, who had his back to them, leaning against the rocky wall of the cove, arms higher than his head, pudgy legs splayed out behind him. Absurdly, she felt a stab of pity for him. There he was, cornered and spread-eagled for frisking like a vicious killer—which he was—and yet it was just poor old fatuous Milt Sawyer, the world's most boring person. Who would there be to listen to his stories about Jackie, and Arnie, and Gerry, and Juli now?

Graham stepped away from her, reached under the waist of his windbreaker, and came up with a clinking pair of handcuffs. (Did he always carry those too?) He jerked one of Milt's arms roughly down from the rock, pressed it behind him against the small of his back, and clicked one of the cuffs onto his wrist.

"Hey," Milt complained, "that's too tight. You better—"

"Shut up," Graham said in a voice like splintering ice.

Milt shut up while his other arm was pulled down and cuffed. In a way he was lucky, Lee thought. If Graham had been one of the old rubber-hose school, Milt would have been in for a very hard time of it.

"Gerald," Graham said, "did you read him his rights?"

"No, sir," Rubio said formally.

"I know my rights," Milt muttered, fatuous to the end. "You don't have to read them to me."

"Read them," Graham told Rubio.

Rubio squirmed. "Uh, I'm afraid I don't—"

With just a touch of irritation Graham pulled a plastic-coated card from his wallet and handed it to him.

The sergeant permitted himself a portentous throat-clearing, like a bewigged judge about to pronounce sentence. "You have the right to remain silent," he read solemnly, and a shiver ran down Lee's spine. "Anything you say can be used against you in a court of law. You have the right at this time . . ."

Within an hour Lee had been in and out of the emergency room of the Peninsula Community Hospital with no more than a dab of antiseptic on her lip and a gauze pad on her arm. ("You're a very lucky girl," the frazzled young doctor had said. "An inch to the right and your playing days would be over.") But it was another long two hours by the time she had made her statement at police headquarters, and another hour later—nine o'clock—before Graham finished up and walked with her to the parking lot.

"You look tired," she said, "but satisfied too."

"That's about it." He turned to her. "You look pretty beat yourself."

"I am," she said sincerely. "What a wonderful, terrible day." She touched his forearm and he stopped. "Graham, you know what I could really use?"

He smiled at her. "Glad to be of service." And in the dark parking lot, surrounded by patrol cars, he enclosed her in his arms again, pressing her head against his chest, softly nuzzling the top of her head.

They stood locked together for a long time, swaying gently, before he finally opened his arms. "How's that?" he murmured. "Better?"

"Much," she said. "But what I had in mind was a pizza."

16

"I'M STILL MIXED up," Lee said, holding a wedge of mushroom pizza at arm's length, trying to sever the gooey strands of mozzarella with her teeth and speak at the same time. They were at Graham's kitchen table, eating from a take-out box. The nearby Straw Hat on Rio Road had been too boisterous and jolly for her frame of mind.

"I don't blame you." Graham licked tomato sauce from his thumb. "Anything in particular?"

"Yes. For one thing Milt took a risk switching those clubs and then sending that letter to the police. That was to make it look as if I killed Kate, right? So why—"

"That's not all he did, apparently. Don't forget that he went out of his way to have dinner with you only an hour or so after he killed her."

Lee paused. "What does that have to do with it?"

"Don't you remember how he was talking—loudly enough for Nick Pittman and others to overhear—about your replacing Kate on the Sawyer endorsement package?"

"Yes, of course, but— Do you mean he was setting me up with a motive? What good would that do him if she was already dead?"

"But nobody knew that then, and even the crime lab can't fix time of death any closer than a couple of hours either way after a little time has passed. Who was to say you didn't run out and do it right after talking to Milt?''

''Sneaky little worm,'' she said with feeling, and reached for her third slice of pizza.

''It also seems to have been Milt who went around telling people you and Kate were so close. Just one more link between the two of you for us coppers to mull over.'' He lifted another wedge from the box. ''Now, what was your question?''

''Well, if he was so busy framing me, why would he want to kill me?''

''He had to. You were right on the edge of putting all the pieces together.''

''Are you kidding? I wasn't anywhere near it.''

''Oh, but you were; you just didn't know it. You told him you were going to see his father on Tuesday and demand the same retainer Kate was getting—a hundred and ten thousand dollars. And that, of course, Milt couldn't risk.''

Lee put down the pizza. ''I don't understand. Couldn't risk what?''

''Look, Kate was getting a hundred and ten thousand, all right, but Ellis Sawyer's company was paying out a hundred and forty thousand.''

''Graham, I'm lost. How—''

''Milt thought it up and worked it out with Farley. Of the extra thirty thousand, twenty-five was going to Milt, five to Farley. And if that got out, Milton Sawyer was going to be in deep trouble, because a pretty plausible scenario would jump out at anyone who thought twice about it: Milt swindles Kate, Kate finds out and threatens to expose him, and he kills her to protect himself.''

Lee took a while digesting this. ''Is that what happened?''

Graham nodded. ''She confronted him with it on the practice tee. Milt claims he never meant to kill her; he just got carried away.

''Do you believe him?''

''Yes, I think I do, but I don't see that it makes much difference. He sure as hell meant to kill you. And Farley.''

''Farley,'' Lee echoed. ''Farley has me confused too. If

it was Milt who killed Kate, why in the world did Farley put that chicken blood on my club?" She shook her head and laughed uneasily. "I can't believe I'm saying these things."

"Well, Farley was in over his head. He didn't know anything about Milt killing Kate, you see. He just knew you were asking uncomfortable questions about her business affairs, and that was his brilliant way of frightening you off before you found out about his part in ripping her off."

"But why did Milt have to kill him?"

"That I'm not sure about yet, but what I think happened is that Farley finally figured out who killed her, or maybe Milt made an error of judgment and told him. Anyway, I think Milt was afraid he'd go to the police and there was only one way to make absolutely sure he didn't. Exit Farley Stratton."

"But why in the world would Farley go to the police? Wouldn't he just get himself in trouble?"

"Sure, for fraud or maybe embezzlement. But I think he was a lot more scared of being implicated in Kate's death. After all, that same murder scenario could apply to him. Making a clean breast of it to the police—and very likely ratting on Milt—was one way of putting himself in the clear."

"God." Lee leaned wearily back in the wooden chair. Her arm throbbed under the bandage, the inside of her mouth stung where it had been bruised, and she felt on the whole as if she'd spent the last couple of days hanging from a tree by her thumbs.

Graham stood and held out his hands to her. "Come on, you look done in. Sit where it's comfortable. Get your feet up. I'll put on some coffee."

Graham's living room was also his study. There was a big work table built into the bay window and ceiling-high shelves filled with well-used books on either side of it. Lee took his advice, leaning back into a nondescript sofa and getting her feet up under her. It was a pleasant room, masculine and uncluttered, with an old oak floor and a few prints of antique maps on the walls. Through the doorway to the kitchen she could see Graham spooning coffee into a filter, whistling softly to himself. Once he looked up to find her watching him and he smiled. No message, no latent meaning, just a brief, open, happy smile.

Lee was happy too, and more than willing to give herself up to being catered to and babied.

"Do you know," she called dreamily to him, "when you showed up on the beach I thought I was imagining you? I couldn't think what you were doing there." She stopped, frowning. "What *were* you doing there? How did you find me?"

"High-class police work, my girl," he said, pouring steaming water into the grounds. He came to the doorway and leaned against it, arms folded. "To tell you the truth, I had it all figured out, but I had the wrong guy. I thought it was Farley. But when he was killed, of course I knew it wasn't him at all."

"That *was* clever."

He lifted a warning eyebrow. "So I did some hard thinking and realized that everything pointed to Milt. He was one of the few people with a connection to both Farley and Kate, and I knew that if anybody from Sawyer was in on the swindle, it would have to be him, because he's the one who works out the details on the contracts. And, of course, I knew he needed money."

"Why 'of course'?"

"Because I'd already laid the groundwork days ago." He shrugged modestly. "Well, Rubio did. He made an estimate of what Milt's high-living, celebrity-toadying lifestyle had to be costing him, then compared it to what Papa was paying him. And there wasn't any comparison. His salary was barely covering his racetrack costs."

He went back into the kitchen. "Like some brandy in your coffee?"

"Mm, yes, please."

He continued speaking while he rummaged in a cupboard for the brandy bottle. "Well, I called the Sawyer company and found out the fees they were paying their other endorsers, and then managed to get hold of three of the endorsers and find how much they were actually getting."

"And there was a difference? They were getting less too?"

"Two of them were, and that was good enough for me. Sorry, no brandy. How about bourbon?"

"Fine," said Lee, who'd never had either in her coffee.

Graham nodded. "The next thing to do was to find out where Milt was, which wasn't too hard because the first place we called was Carmel Point, figuring he'd been at the tournament. That was around four-thirty, and they told us he was out on the course right that minute."

He splashed bourbon into each mug, then stirred in a little sugar. "I asked if they knew where you were, and they said they thought you were out there too."

"I was, but not with him."

"But I didn't know that and the possibility scared the absolute hell out of me. I never moved so fast in my life."

"Thank you," she said softly.

He looked up with a crooked smile. "Well, Jesus, do you know how much paperwork another homicide would have meant? Anyway, inside of ten minutes we were reconnoitering the course—"

"In the helicopter? That was you?"

"That was me." He came in with a coffee mug in each hand. "Hey, we make a great team, don't we?"

"Not bad. I like the arrangement. I do the brainwork; you take care of the physical stuff at the end."

He laughed. "No, I think it's the other way around. I'm the one who figured out it was Milt—but when I finally caught up with him you'd outwrestled him, taken away his gun, and were giving a very convincing impression of being about to plug him. Here. Drink it slowly; there's a double shot in it."

Obediently Lee took a tiny swallow, sighing with pleasure at the ribbon of warmth that flowed down to her stomach. Graham stood quietly watching her.

"I like seeing you here," he said.

"I like being here." Her hand went to her swollen mouth. "I must look awful, like a chipmunk."

"I like chipmunks." He sat down in an armchair beside her. "You'll be back here in a few weeks?" he said. "When you play in San Jose?"

"Uh-huh." She was ridiculously pleased that he had mentioned it again.

"I was thinking," he said. "Maybe we don't need to wait that long. I could probably manage some time off by Wednesday, and, well, maybe I could fly up to Reno and spend a few days. If I wouldn't be in your way, that is." He hesitated, looking down at his mug. "I mean, I know it's short notice, but . . . Well, if you have other plans, just say so. I mean . . . What are you laughing at?"

At you, she wanted to say. Because it's so utterly charming to see a competent, verbal, impressively self-assured man—the same one who could point a .38 at someone and growl "Freeze!" so uncompromisingly—fumbling over his words like a nervous teenager asking for his first date.

"I'm laughing because I'm happy," she said. And that was true too; that was most assuredly true. "I would love it if you came up to Reno." And suddenly she was embarrassed too.

"Good," he said. He got down to one knee to kiss her on the uninjured side of her mouth. Three separate times, very gently.

"I should warn you," he said, "that all this gingerly and sensitive behavior may be misleading you. I am a man of violent and uncontrollable passions. At the appropriate times, of course."

"I'm glad to hear it," she said with her hands clasped around his neck, her wrists resting on his shoulders. "Have I thanked you yet for saving my life today?"

"No—but I was under the impression it was Milt's life I was saving." He smiled. "Not that he bothered to thank me either."

They looked into each other's eyes for a long, sweet moment, the first time they'd allowed themselves the luxury.

"Graham, can I use your telephone?"

Understandably he seemed surprised. "The telephone? Sure, it's in the kitchen." He unclasped her hands and pulled her up.

Peg answered on the second ring.

"Peg, I was thinking—"

"Lee?" she interrupted excitedly. "I'm glad you called. I've finally got it figured out. It's Farley. It has to be. He—"

"It's not Farley," Lee said.

"But let me tell you what my contact found out. Farley was cheating Kate out—"

"Farley's dead."

There was a long silence. Lee heard Peg breathe in, then out. "You mean *killed* dead?"

"Killed dead. Murdered."

Peg's deep voice dropped another half-octave. "My God, then who—"

"Milt Sawyer."

"Milt? No, no, that's—"

"It's Milt. He tried to kill me too."

"*You?* Lee, what's going on? Are you—"

"I'm all right now. I'm with Graham. And Milt's locked up."

"But . . . but . . . I mean, but . . ."

"Peg, I've had a heck of a day. I'm really bushed. I'll tell you all about it tomorrow, okay? I promise. Every detail."

"All right, if that's what you want," Peg said reluctantly, "but don't expect me to get any sleep. I'll see you at eight then?"

Lee cleared her throat. "Uh, well, that's what I was calling about," she said, and lowered her voice with a sidewise glance into the living room. "I was thinking about that, you know, and I, uh . . . well, maybe lunch would be better after all."

About the Author

AARON ELKINS, the author of the Edgar-winning *Old Bones*, teams up with his wife, CHARLOTTE, to fashion this lighthearted story (yes, murder *can* be lighthearted)—a fictional look at the less-glamorous side of a golf tour. And they give us a golfing heroine whom readers (along with Police Lieutenant Graham Sheldon) will be thoroughly enchanted with.